SILVER LAKE

R.M. BALLANTYNE

Frontispiece by John Betancourt. Based on a painting.

SILVER LAKE

R.M. Ballantyne

WILDSIDE PRESS

SILVER LAKE

INTRODUCTION

Robert Michael Ballantyne (1825–1894) was a Scottish author who published more than 100 books. He was also an accomplished artist and exhibited some of his water-colours at the Royal Scottish Academy.

Ballantyne was born in Edinburgh, the ninth of ten children (and the youngest son), to Alexander and Anne Ballantyne. His father was a newspaper editor and printer in the family firm of "Ballantyne & Co" based at Paul's Works on the Canongate. His uncle, James Ballantyne, was the printer for Scottish author Sir Walter Scott. A banking crisis in 1825 resulted in the collapse of the Ballantyne printing business the following year with debts of £130,000,which led to a decline in the family's fortunes.

Robert Ballantyne went to Canada at the age of 16 and spent five years working for the Hudson's Bay Company. He traded with the local Native Americans for furs, which required him to travel by canoe and sleigh to the areas occupied by the modern-day provinces of Manitoba, Ontario, and Quebec—experiences that formed the basis of his novel *Snowflakes and Sunbeams* (1856). His longing for family and home during that period impressed him to start writing letters to his mother. Ballantyne recalled in his autobiographical *Personal Reminiscences in Book Making* (1893) that "To this long-letter writing I attribute whatever small amount of facility in composition I may have acquired."

In 1847 Ballantyne returned to Scotland to discover that his father had died. He published his first book the following year, *Hudson's Bay: or, Life in the Wilds of North America*, and for some time was employed by the publishers Messrs Constable. In 1856 he gave up business to focus on his literary career and began the series of adventure stories for the young with which his name is popularly associated.

The Young Fur-Traders (1856), *The Coral Island* (1857), *The World of Ice* (1859), *Ungava: a Tale of Eskimo Land* (1857), *The Dog*

Crusoe (1860), *The Lighthouse* (1865), *Fighting the Whales* (1866), *Deep Down* (1868), *The Pirate City* (1874), *Erling the Bold* (1869), *The Settler and the Savage* (1877), and more than 100 other books followed in regular succession, his rule being to write as far as possible from personal knowledge of the scenes he described. *The Gorilla Hunters: A tale of the wilds of Africa* (1861) shares three characters with The Coral Island: Jack Martin, Ralph Rover and Peterkin Gay. Here Ballantyne relied factually on Paul du Chaillu's Exploration in Equatorial Guinea, which had appeared early in the same year.

The Coral Island remains the most popular of the Ballantyne novels still read and remembered today, but because of a mistake he made in that book—he gave an incorrect thickness of coconut shells—he prioritized research on his subjects for later books. For instance, he spent time living with the lighthouse keepers at the Bell Rock before writing *The Lighthouse*, and he spent time with the tin miners of Cornwall while researching *Deep Down*.

In 1866 he married Jane Grant, with whom he had three sons and three daughters. He spent his later years in Harrow, London, before moving to Italy for the sake of his health, possibly suffering from undiagnosed Ménière's disease. He died in Rome in 1894 and was buried in the Protestant Cemetery there.

One of the young men influenced by Ballantyne's novels was Robert Louis Stevenson (1850–94). Stevenson was so impressed with the story of *The Coral Island* (1857) that he based portions of his most famous book, *Treasure Island* (1881), on themes found in Ballantyne's classic novel.

—Karl Wurf
Rockville, Maryland

CHAPTER I.

The Hunters.

It was on a cold winter morning long ago, that Robin Gore, a bold hunter of the backwoods of America, entered his parlour and sat him down to breakfast.

Robin's parlour was also his dining-room, and his drawing-room, besides being his bedroom and his kitchen. In fact, it was the only room in his wooden hut, except a small apartment, opening off it, which was a workshop and lumber-room.

Robin's family consisted of himself, and his wife, and his son Roy, who was twelve years of age — and his daughter Nelly, who was eight, or thereabout. In addition to these, his household comprised a nephew, Walter and an Irishman, Larry O'Dowd. The former was tall, strong, fearless, and twenty. The latter was stout, short, powerful, and forty.

The personal history of Robin Gore, to the point at which we take it up, runs briefly thus: —

He had been born in a backwood's settlement, had grown up and married in the little hamlet in which he had been born, and hunted around it contentedly until he was forty years of age. But, as population increased, he became restive. He disliked restraint; resolved to take his wife and family into the wilderness and after getting his nephew and an Irish adventurer to agree to accompany him, carried his resolution into effect.

He travelled several hundreds of miles into the woods — beyond the most remote settlement — built three wooden huts, surrounded them with a tall stockade, set up a flagstaff in the centre thereof, and styled the whole affair, "Fort Enterprise."

"I'm sorry to bring you to such a lonesome spot, Molly, my dear," said Robin, as he sat on the trunk of a fallen tree on the afternoon of the day on which he arrived at the scene of his future home; "it'll be rayther tryin' at first, but you'll soon get used to it, and we won't be bothered hereaway wi' all the new-fangled notions o' settlement folk. We'll dwell in the free wilderness, where there are no tyrannical laws to hamper a man, an' no nonsensical customs to fix the fashion of his coat an' leggins. Besides, you'll have Roy an' Nelly an' Walter an' Larry to keep you company, lass, not to mention our neighbours to look in upon now and again."

"Very true, Robin," replied the wife, "I have no doubt it will be quite cheery and homelike in course of time."

She looked out upon the broad bosom of the lake which lay before the site of their forest home, and sighed. It was evident that Mrs. Gore had a strong partiality for the laws and customs which her husband abhorred.

The "neighbours" to whom Robin referred lived in a leather tent twenty miles distant from the Fort. They were an Indian, named "The Black Swan," his wife, named "The White Swan," and a half-caste trapper, whose proper name was unknown to all save himself. His cognomen in the wilderness was "Slugs," a name which originated in his frequent use of clipped pieces of lead instead of shot in the loading of his gun.

But to return to the point from which we started: —

It was on a cold winter morning that Robin Gore entered his parlour and sat him down to breakfast.

It was not only cold — very cold; colder than ever was experienced in our favoured British isles — but it was also very dark. Robin had risen before daybreak in order to visit his traps, and shoot some game as early in the day as possible. The larder chanced to be nearly empty that day, a fact which was all the more to be regretted that it was New Year's day, and, as Robin remarked, "that day didn't occur more than once in the year." This statement Larry O'Dowd disputed, affirming that it occurred "at laste twice ivery year — wance at the beginnin' an' wance at the end of it!"

"Come along, lad," said Robin, trimming the candle as his nephew Walter entered, "we'll ha' to make the most of our time today, for we dine at sharp five P.M., an' our dinner — leastwise the most of it — is at this moment alive an' kickin', if it's not sleepin', in the forest, and has got to be found and shot yet. Hallo! boy, where are *you* bound for?"

"For the woods, father, with you and Walter," replied his son Roy, sitting down and coolly helping himself to a portion of bear's meat with which the hunter was regaling himself.

"Nonsense, boy," said Robin, somewhat gruffly.

"You'll not be able to keep up with us," added Walter, "for we've little time before us, an' a long way to go."

"If I break down I can turn back," retorted Roy.

"Very good; please yourself," said Robin in a tone of indifference, although his glance seemed to indicate that he was not sorry to see his boy determined to attempt an expedition which he knew from experience would be very trying to a lad of his years.

Breakfast over, the three hunters clothed themselves in habiliments suitable to the climate — leathern coats and trousers which were impervious to the wind; cloth leggings to keep the snow from the trousers; leather mocassins, or shoes with three pairs of blanket socks inside of them; fur-caps with ear-pieces; leather mittens with an apartment for the fingers and a separate chamber for the thumb, powder-horns, shot-pouches, guns, and snowshoes. These latter were light wooden frames, netted across with deerskin threads, about five feet long and upwards of a foot wide. The shoes were of this enormous size, in order that they might support the wearers on the surface of the snow, which was, on an average, four feet deep in the woods. They were clumsy to look at, but not so difficult to walk in as one might suppose.

In silence the three hunters entered the dark woods in front of Fort Enterprise. Robin went first and beat the track, Walter followed in his footsteps, Roy brought up the rear. The father sank about six inches at every step, but the snow which fell upon his snowshoes was so fine and dry, owing to the intense frost, that it fell through the net-work of the shoes like dust. Walter and Roy, treading in the footsteps, had less labour in walking, but Walter, being almost as strong as his uncle, took his turn at beating the track every two hours.

Through the woods they went, over mound and hollow, across frozen swamp and plain, through brush and break, until near noon, when they halted for rest and refreshment. While Walter cut firewood, Robin and Roy cleared away the snow, using their snowshoes as shovels, and prepared their meal. It was simple; a few mouthfuls of dried meat and a tin can of hot tea — the backwoodsman's greatest luxury, next to his pipe. It was short, too. Half an hour sufficed to prepare and consume it.

"Let's see, now, what we have got," said Robin, counting the game before resuming the march.

"More than enough," said Walter, lighting his pipe for a hurried whiff, "ten brace of white grouse, four rabbits, six red foxes and a black one, and two wolves. We can't eat all that."

"Surely we won't eat the foxes and wolves!" cried Roy, laughing.

"Not till we're starvin'," replied his father. "Come, let's go on — are ye tired, lad?"

"Fresh as Walter," said the boy, proudly.

"Well, we won't try you too much. We'll just take a sweep round by the Wolf's Glen, an' look at the traps there — after which make for home and have our New Year's dinner. Go ahead, Walter, and beat the track; it is your turn this time."

Without speaking, Walter slipped his feet into the lines of his snowshoes, extinguished his pipe, and led the way once more through the pathless forest.

CHAPTER II.

The Starved Indian.

In the depths of the same forest, and not far from the locality to which we have introduced our reader, a Red Indian was dragging his limbs wearily along over the untrodden snow.

The attenuated frame of this son of the soil, his hollow cheeks and glaring eyeballs, his belt drawn with extreme tightness round his waist, to repress the gnawings of hunger, as well as his enfeebled gait, proved that he was approaching the last stage of starvation.

For many weeks Wapaw had been travelling in the woods, guided on his way by the stars, and by those slight and delicate signs of the wilderness — such as the difference of thickness in the bark on the north, from that on the south side of a tree — which are perceptible only to the keen eye of an Indian, or a white man whose life has been spent in the wilderness.

But Wapaw was a very different man when he quitted his tribe from what he was at the time we introduce him to our reader. Strong, wiry, upright, and lithe as a panther, he left his wigwam and his wife, and turned his face towards the rising sun; but the season was a severe one, and game was scarce; from the very beginning of his journey he had found it difficult to supply himself with a sufficiency of food. Towards the middle of it he was on short allowance, and much reduced in strength; and now near its termination, he was, as we have said, almost in the last stage of starvation.

Fort Enterprise was Wapaw's goal. He had never been there before, but from the description of the place and its locality, given by those of his kindred who had visited Robin Gore, he was able to direct his march with unerring certainty towards it. Of course, as he drew near to it he could not ascertain his exact distance — whether he was a day or several days' journey off — but from the tracks of Robin's snowshoes, which he crossed more than once, he guessed that he was nearing the Fort, and pushed on with renewed hope and energy.

Robin, however, was an active hunter. He often made long and rapid marches from his lonely dwelling — sometimes staying away a week or two at a time even in winter; so that Wapaw thought himself nearer Fort Enterprise than he really was when he first discovered the bold hunter's tracks. When, at length, he did arrive at less than a day's journey from the Fort, he was not aware of its close proximity, and, having tasted nothing whatever for two days, he felt the approach of that terrible state of exhaustion which precedes death.

It was a somewhat stormy day when the poor Indian's strength finally broke down. Hitherto he had pushed forward with some degree of hope, but on the morning of this day a broken branch caught his snowshoe and tripped him. At any other time the fall would have been a trifle, but in his weak condition it acted like the last straw which breaks the camel's back. Wapaw rose with difficulty, and brushing the snow from his eyes, looked earnestly at his snowshoes, well knowing that if they had been broken in the fall his power of advancing would have been taken away and his fate sealed, for he had neither strength nor energy left to repair them. They were uninjured, however; so he once more attempted to stagger on.

A slight rising ground lay before him. To ascend this was a labour so great that he almost sank in the midst of it. He reached the top, however, and gazed eagerly before him. He had gazed thus at the top of every rising ground that he had reached during the last two days, in the hope of seeing some sign of the Fort.

A deep sigh escaped him as he rested his hands on the muzzle of his gun, and his grave countenance was overspread with a look of profound melancholy. For the first time in his life, the once stout and active Wapaw had reached the point of giving way to despair. A wide open plain stretched out before him. The cold wind was howling wildly across it, driving the keen snow-drift before it in whirling clouds. Even a strong man might have shrunk from exposing himself on such a plain and to such a blast on that bitter arctic day. Wapaw felt that in his case to cross it would be certain death; so, with the calm philosophy of a Red Indian, he made up his mind to lay him down and die!

His manner of preparing for his end was somewhat singular. Turning aside into the woods, he set about making an encampment with as much vigour as he could summon up. Clearing away the snow from the roots of a large spreading pine-tree, he strewed branches on the ground, and thus made a rude couch. On this he spread his blanket. Then he cut some firewood with the axe that hung at his side, and soon kindled, by means of flint, steel, and tinder, a good fire. Seating himself before the warm blaze, the exhausted man rested awhile, with his legs drawn together and his head resting on his knees.

He sat so long thus that he nearly fell asleep. Presently he roused himself, and proceeded to make a close examination of his wallet and firebag — the latter being a beautifully ornamented pouch, which Indians and fur-traders wear at their belts, for the purpose of containing the materials for producing fire, besides pipes and tobacco.

Poor Wapaw had already searched his wallet and firebag twice, without finding a crumb of food or a morsel of tobacco. He knew well that they were empty, yet he turned them inside out, and examined the seams and corners with as much earnestness as if he really expected to find relief from his sufferings there.

There was no expression of pain on the red man's face — only a look of profound melancholy.

He laid aside the firebag after a little while, and then quietly drew his knife, and cut a piece of leather from the skirt of his hunting coat.

The leather had been dried and smoked, and contained no substance whatever that could sustain life. Wapaw was aware of this — nevertheless he singed a portion of it until it was reduced almost to ashes, and mingling a little snow with this, ate it greedily.

Then, raising his eyes to the sky with a long earnest gaze, he sat immovable, until the sinking fire and the increasing cold recalled his wandering faculties.

There was a wild, glassy look about the Indian's eyes now, which probably resulted from exhaustion. He seemed to struggle several times to rouse himself before he succeeded; shuddering with intense cold, he crept to the little pile of firewood, and placed several billets on the fire, which speedily blazed up again, and the dying man cowered over it, regardless of the smoke which ever and anon wreathed round his drooping head.

In a few minutes Wapaw started up as if new energy had been infused into him. He placed his gun, axe, firebag, and powder-horn by themselves on the ground; then he wrapped himself in his blanket and lay slowly down beside them with his feet towards the fire. For a few minutes he lay on his back, gazing earnestly upwards, while his lips moved slowly, but no sound issued from them. Then he turned wearily on his side, and, covering his head with the blanket and turning his face towards the ground, he resigned himself to death.

But God had ordained that, at that time, the red man should not die.

About the time when he lay down, our hunters emerged upon the plain which had caused the Indian to despair.

"It's of no use goin' farther," observed Robin, as he and his companions stood at the edge of the forest and looked across the plain; "the wind blows too hard, and the drift is keen; besides there ain't much to be got hereaway, even in seasons of plenty."

"Father! is that smoke risin' over the bluff yonder?" asked Roy, pointing with his finger as he spoke.

"No doubt of it, lad."

"Indians, may be," said Walter.

Robin shook his head. "Don't think so," said he, "for the redskins don't often come to see me at this time o' the year. But we'll go see; an' look to your primin', lads — if it's a war-party we'll ha' to fight, mayhap, if we don't run."

The three hunters crossed the plain in the teeth of the howling drift, and cautiously approached the bluff referred to by Roy, and from behind which the smoke ascended.

"It's a camp fire," whispered Robin, as he glanced back at his companions, "but I see no one there. They must have just left the place."

There was a shade of anxiety in the hunter's voice as he spoke, for he thought of Fort Enterprise, its defenceless condition, and the possibility of the Indians having gone thither.

"They can't have gone to the Fort," said Walter, "else we should have seen their tracks on the way hither."

"Come," said Robin, stepping forward quickly, "we can see their tracks now, anyhow, and follow them up, and if they lead to the Fort."

The hunter did not finish his sentence, for at that moment he caught sight of the recumbent form of Wapaw in the camp.

"Hist! A redskin alone, and asleep! Well, I never did 'xpect to see that."

"Mayhap, he's a decoy-duck," suggested Walter. "Better look sharp out."

Robin and Roy heeded not the caution. They at once went forward, and the father lifted the blanket from the Indian's head.

"Dead!" exclaimed Roy, in a solemn tone.

"Not yet, lad! but I do b'lieve the poor critter's a'most gone wi' starvation. Come, bestir you, boys — rouse up the fire, and boil the kettle."

Walter and Roy did not require a second bidding. The kettle was ere long singing on a blazing fire. The Indian's limbs were chafed and warmed; a can of hot tea was administered, and Wapaw soon revived sufficiently to look up and thank his deliverers.

"Now, as good luck has it, I chanced to leave my hand-sled at the Wolf's Glen. Go, fetch it, Roy," said Robin.

The lad set off at once, and, as the glen was not far distant, soon returned with a flat wooden sledge, six feet long by eighteen inches broad, on which trappers are wont to pack their game in winter. On this sledge Wapaw was firmly tied, and dragged by the hunters to Fort Enterprise.

"Hast got a deer, father?" cried little Nelly, as she bounded in advance of her mother to meet the returning party.

"No, Nelly — 'tis dearer game than that."

"What? a redskin!" exclaimed Dame Gore in surprise; "is he dead?"

"No, nor likely to die," said Robin, "he's in a starvin' state though, an'll be none the worse of a bit of our New Year's dinner. Here is game enough for one meal an' more; come, lass, get it ready as fast as may be."

So saying the bold hunter passed through the Fort gate, dragging the red man behind him.

CHAPTER III.

Preparations for a Feast.

"Why so grave, Robin?" inquired Mrs. Gore, when her husband returned to the parlour after seeing Wapaw laid in a warm corner of the kitchen, and committed to the care of Larry O'Dowd.

"Molly, my dear, it's of no use concealin' things from you, 'cause when bad luck falls we must just face it. This Injun — Wapaw, he calls himself — tells me he has com'd here a-purpose, as fast as he could, to say that his tribe have resolved to attack me, burn the Fort, kill all the men, and carry you off into slavery."

"God help me! can this be true?"

"True enough, I don't doubt, 'cause Wapaw has the face of an honest man, and I believe in faces. He says some of the worst men of his tribe are in power just now; that they want the contents of my store without paying for them; that he tried to get them to give up the notion, but failed. On seeing that they were bent on it, he said he was going off to hunt, and came straight here to warn me. He says they talked of starting for the Fort two days after he did, and that he pushed on as fast as he could travel, so it's not likely they'll be here for two or three days yet. I'll get ready for them, hows'ever, and when the reptiles do come they'll meet with a warm reception, I warrant them; meanwhile, do you go and get dinner ready. We won't let such varmints interfere with our New Year's feast."

While Robin's wife went to her larder, his children were in the kitchen tending the Indian with earnest solicitude, and Larry was preparing a little soup for him.

"Do you like rabbit soup?" asked Nelly, kneeling beside the pallet of pine branches on which Wapaw lay.

The Indian smiled, and said something in his native tongue.

"Sure he don't onderstan' ye," exclaimed Larry, as he bustled in an energetic way amongst his pots and pans.

"Let me try him with Cree," said Roy, kneeling beside his sister, "I know a little — a *very* little Cree."

Roy tried his "very little Cree," but without success.

"It's o' no use," he said, "father must talk to him, for *he* knows every language on earth, I believe."

Roy's idea of the number of languages "on earth" was very limited.

"Och! don't bother him, see, here is a lingo that every wan onderstan's," cried Larry, carrying a can of hot soup towards Wapaw.

"Oh, let me! *do* let me!" cried Nelly, jumping up and seizing the can.

"Be all manes," said Larry, resigning it.

The child once more knelt by the side of the Indian and held the can to him, while he conveyed the soup to his lips with a trembling, unsteady hand. The eyes of the poor man glittered as he gazed eagerly at the food, which he ate with the avidity of a half-famished wolf.

His nurses looked on with great satisfaction, and when Wapaw glanced up from time to time in their faces, he was advised to continue his meal with nods and smiles of goodwill.

Great preparations were made for the dinner of that New Year's Day. Those who "dwell at home at ease" have no idea of the peculiar feelings with which the world's wanderers hail the season of Christmas and New Year. Surrounded as they usually are by strange scenes, and ignorant as they are of what friends at home are doing or thinking, they lay hold of this season as being one point at least in the circle of the year in which they can unite with the home circle, and, at the *same time*, commemorate with them the birth of the blessed Saviour of mankind, and think with them of absent friends. Much, therefore, as the "happy" season is made of in the "old country," it is made more of, if possible, in the colonies; especially on the outskirts of the world, where the adventurous and daring have pitched their tents.

Of course Robin Gore and his household did not think of the "old country," for they were descendants of settlers; but they had imbibed the spirit of the old country from their forefathers, and thought of those well-remembered friends whom they had left behind them in the settlements.

Notwithstanding the delay caused by the conveying of Wapaw to the Fort, the hunters had walked so fast that there was still some time to spare before dinner should be ready.

Roy resolved to devote this time to a ramble in the woods with his sister Nelly. Accordingly the two put on their snowshoes, and, merely saying to their mother that they were going to take a run in the woods, set forth.

Now, it must be known that Mrs. Gore had looked forward to New Year's Day dinner with great interest and much anxiety. There was a general feeling of hilarity and excitement among the male members of the self-exiled family that extended itself to the good woman, and induced her to resolve that the entire household should have what Walter styled a "rare blow-out!" During the whole morning she had been busy with the preparation of the various dishes, among which were a tart made of cloudberry jam, a salt goose, and a lump of bear's ham, besides the rabbits and ptarmigan which had been shot that day.

"That's the way to do it, Molly," cried Robin, as he opened the door and peeped in upon his wife during the height and heat of her culinary labours; "keep the pot bilin', my dear, and don't spare the butter this day. It only comes once a year, you know."

"Twice," muttered Larry in a low voice, as he stirred the contents of a large pot which hung over the fire.

"And see that you look after Wapaw," continued Robin. "Don't give him too much at first, it'll hurt him."

"No fear of that," replied Larry, "he's got so much a'ready that he couldn't howld another morsel av he was to try."

"Well, well, take care of him, anyhow," said Robin, with a laugh; "meanwhile I'll go see after the defences o' the Fort, and make all snug."

By dint of unwearied perseverance the dinner was cooked, and then it occurred to Robin to ask where the children were, but no one could tell, so the hunter remarked quietly that they would "doubtless make their appearance in a short while."

Gradually the dinner reached that interesting point which is usually styled "ready to dish." Whereupon Robin again asked where the children were. Still no one could tell, so he said he would go out and hail them. Loudly and long did the hunter call, but no one answered; then he made a rapid search in and about the Fort, but they were not to be found. Moreover, a snow-storm had begun to set in, and the drift rendered it difficult to distinguish tracks in the snow.

At last the day's labours were brought to a close. Dinner was served, and smoked invitingly on the table. The party only awaited the return of Robin with the children. In a few minutes Robin entered hastily.

"Molly," said he, in a tone of anxiety, "the foolish things have gone into the woods, I think. Come, lads, we must hunt them down. It's snowin' hard, so we've no time to lose."

Walter and Larry at once put on their capotes, fur-caps, and snow-shoes, and sallied forth, leaving Mrs. Gore seated alone, and in a state of deep anxiety, by the side of her untasted New Year's Day dinner.

CHAPTER IV.

Lost in the Snow.

When Roy and Nelly set out for a ramble, they had at first no intention of going beyond their usual haunts in the woods around the Fort; but Roy had been inspirited by his successful march that day with his father and Walter, and felt inclined to show Nelly some new scenes to which they had not, up to that time, dared to penetrate together.

The snow-storm, already referred to, had commenced gradually. When the children set forth on their ramble only a few flakes were falling, but they had not been away half an hour when snow fell so thickly that they could not see distinctly more than a few yards ahead of them. There was no wind, however, so they continued to advance, rather pleased than otherwise with the state of things.

"Oh, I *do* like to see falling snow," cried Nelly, with a burst of animation.

"So do I," said Roy, looking back at his sister with a bright smile, "and I like it best when it comes down thick and heavy, in big flakes, on a *very* calm day, don't you?"

"Yes, oh it's so nice," responded Nelly sympathetically.

They paused for minutes to shake some of the snow from their garments, and beat their hands together, for their fingers were cold, and to laugh boisterously, for their hearts were merry. Then they resumed their march, Roy beating the track manfully and Nelly following in his footsteps.

In passing beneath a tall fir-tree Roy chanced to touch a twig. The result was literally overwhelming, for in a moment he was almost buried in snow, to the unutterable delight of his sister, who stood screaming with laughter as the unfortunate boy struggled to disentomb himself.

In those northern wilds, where snow falls frequently and in great abundance, masses are constantly accumulating on the branches of trees, particularly on the pines, on the broad flat branches of which these masses attain to considerable size. A slight touch is generally sufficient to bring these down, but, being soft, they never do any injury worth mentioning.

When Roy had fairly emerged from the snow he joined his sister in the laugh, but suddenly he stopped, and his face became very grave.

"What's the matter?" asked Nelly, with an anxious look.

"My snowshoe's broken," said Roy.

There was greater cause for anxiety on account of this accident than the reader is perhaps aware of. It may be easily understood that in a country where the snow averages four feet in depth, no one can walk half-a-mile without snowshoes without being thoroughly exhausted; on the other hand, a man can walk thirty or forty miles a day by means of snowshoes.

"Can't you mend it?" asked Nelly.

Roy, who had been carefully examining the damaged shoe, shook his head.

"I've nothing here to do it with; besides, it's an awful smash. I must just try to scramble home the best way I can. Come, it's not very far, we'll only be a bit late for dinner."

The snowshoe having been bandaged, after a fashion, with a pocket-handkerchief, the little wanderers began to retrace their steps; but this was now a matter of extreme difficulty, owing to the quantity of snow which had fallen and almost obliterated the tracks. The broken shoe, also, was constantly giving way, so that ere long the children became bewildered as well as anxious, and soon lost the track of their outward march altogether. To make matters worse, the wind began to blow clouds of snow-drift into their faces, compelling them to seek the denser parts of the forest for shelter.

They wandered on, however, in the belief that they were drawing nearer home every step, and Roy, whose heart was stout and brave, cheered up his sister's spirit so much that she began to feel quite confident their troubles would soon be over.

Presently all their hopes were dashed to the ground by their suddenly emerging upon an open space, close to the very spot where the snow-mass had fallen on Roy's head. After the first feeling of alarm and disappointment had subsided, Roy plucked up heart and encouraged

Nelly by pointing out to her that they had at all events recovered their old track, which they would be very careful not to lose sight of again.

Poor Nelly whimpered a little, partly from cold and hunger as well as from disappointment, as she listened to her brother's words; then she dried her eyes and said she was ready to begin again. So they set off once more. But the difficulty of discerning the track, if great at first, was greater now, because the falling and drifting snow had well-nigh covered it up completely. In a very few minutes Roy stopped, and, confessing that he had lost it again, proposed to return once more to their starting point to try to recover it. Nelly agreed, for she was by this time too much fatigued and alarmed to have any will of her own, and was quite ready to do whatever she was told without question.

After wandering about for nearly an hour in this state of uncertainty, Roy at last stopped, and, putting his arm round his sister's waist, said that he had lost himself altogether! Poor Nelly, whose heart had been gradually sinking, fairly broke down; she hid her face in her brother's bosom, and wept.

"Come now, don't do that, dear Nell," said Roy, tenderly, "I'll tell you what we shall do — we'll camp in the snow! We have often done it close to the house, you know, for fun, so we'll do it now in earnest."

"But it's so dark and cold," sobbed Nelly, looking round with a shudder into the dark recesses of the forest, which were by that time enshrouded by the gathering shades of night; "and I'm *so* hungry too! Oh me! what *shall* we do?"

"Now *don't* get so despairing," urged Roy, whose courage rose in proportion as his sister's sank; "it's not such an awful business after all, for father is sure to scour the woods in search of us, an' if we only get a comfortable encampment made, an' a roarin' fire kindled, why, we'll sit beside it an' tell stories till they find us. They'll be sure to see the fire, you know, so come — let's to work."

Roy said this so cheerfully that the child felt a little comforted, dried her eyes, and said she would "help to make the camp."

This matter of making an encampment in the snow, although laborious work, was by no means a novelty to these children of the backwoods. They had often been taught how to do it by Cousin Walter and Larry O'Dowd, and had made "playing at camps" their chief amusement in fine winter days. When, therefore, they found themselves compelled to "camp-out" from necessity, neither of them was at a loss how to proceed. Roy drew a circle in the snow, about three yards in diameter, at the foot of a large tree, and then both set to work to dig a hole in this space, using their snowshoes as shovels. It took an hour's hard work to reach the ground, and when they did so the piled-up snow all round raised the walls of this hole to the height of about six feet.

"Now for bedding," cried Roy, scrambling over the walls of their camp and going into the woods in search of a young pine-tree, while Nelly sat down on the ground to rest after her toil.

It was a dark night, and the woods were so profoundly obscured, that Roy had to grope about for some time before he found a suitable tree. Cutting it down with the axe which always hung at his girdle, he returned to camp with it on his shoulder, and cut off the small soft branches, which Nelly spread over the ground to the depth of nearly half a foot. This "pine-brush," as it is called, formed a soft elastic couch.

The fire was the next business. Again Roy went into the bush and gathered a large bundle of dry branches.

"Now, Nelly, do you break a lot of the small twigs," said Roy, "and I'll strike a light."

He pulled his firebag from his belt as he spoke, and drew from it flint, steel, and tinder. No one ever travels in the wilds of which we write without such means of procuring fire. Roy followed the example of his elder companions in carrying a firebag, although he did not, like them, carry tobacco and pipe in it.

Soon the bright sparks that flew from the flint caught on the tinder. This was placed in a handful of dry grass, and whirled rapidly round until it was fanned into a flame. Nelly had prepared another handful of dry grass with small twigs above it. The light was applied, the fire leaped up, more sticks were piled on, and at last the fire roared upward, sending bright showers of sparks into the branches overhead, lighting the white walls of the camp with a glow that caused them to sparkle as with millions of gems, and filling the hearts of the children with a sensation of comfort and gladness, while they stood before the blaze and warmed themselves, rubbing their hands and laughing with glee.

No one, save those who have experienced it, can form any conception of the cheering effect of a fire in the heart of a dark wood at night. Roy and Nelly quite forgot their lost condition for a short time, in the enjoyment of the comforting heat and the bright gladsome blaze. The brother cut firewood until he was rendered almost breathless, the sister heaped on the wood until the fire roared and leaped high above their heads. Strange though it may appear to some, the snow did not melt. The weather was too cold for that; only a little of that which was nearest the fire melted – the snow walls remained hard frozen all round. Roy soon sat down to rest, as close to the fire as he could without getting scorched; then Nelly seated herself by his side and nestled her head in his breast. There they sat, telling stories and gazing at the fire, and waiting for "father to come."

Meanwhile Robin and his comrade ranged the forest far and near in desperate anxiety. But it was a wide and wild country. The children had wandered far away; a high ridge of land hid their fire from view. Moreover, Robin, knowing the children's usual haunts, had chanced to go off in the wrong direction. When night set in the hunters returned to Fort Enterprise to procure ammunition and provisions, in order to commence a more thorough and prolonged search. Poor Mrs. Gore still sat beside the cold and untasted feast, and there the hunters left her, while they once more plunged into the pathless wilderness to search for the lost ones on that luckless New Year's Day.

CHAPTER V.

Carried Off.

While Robin Gore and his companions were anxiously searching the woods around Fort Enterprise for the lost children, a war-party of savages was making its way swiftly towards the Fort.

A chief of the Indians, named Hawk, who was a shrewd as well as a bad man, had suspected Wapaw's intentions in quitting the camp of his people alone and in such unnecessary haste. This man had great influence over his fellows, and easily prevailed on them to set off on their murderous expedition against the Fort of the "palefaces" without delay.

Being well supplied with food, they travelled faster than their starving comrade, and almost overtook him. They finally encamped within a short distance of the Fort the day after Wapaw's arrival, and prepared to assault it early next morning.

"If the wicked skunk has got there before us," said Hawk to his fellows, as they prepared to set out before daybreak, "the palefaces will be ready for us, and we may as well go back to our wigwams at once; but if that badger's whelp has been slow of foot, we shall hang the scalps of the pale-faces at our belts, and eat their food this day."

The polite titles above used by Hawk were meant to refer to Wapaw.

Indians are not naturally loquacious. No reply was made to Hawk's remark, except that one man with a blackened face, and a streak of red ochre down the bridge of his nose, said, "Ho!" and another with an equally black face, and three red streaks on each of his cheeks, said, "Hum!" as the war-party put on their snowshoes and prepared to start.

They had not gone far when Hawk came to a sudden pause, and stood transfixed and motionless like a dark statue. His comrades also stopped abruptly and crouched. No question was asked, but Hawk pointed to a spark of fire, which every Indian in the band had observed the instant their leader had paused. Silently they crept forward, with guns cocked and arrows fitted to the bowstrings, until they all stood round an encampment where the fire was still smouldering, and in the centre of which lay a little boy and girl, fast asleep and shuddering with cold.

Poor Roy and Nelly had told each other stories until their eyes would not remain open; then they fell asleep, despite their efforts to keep awake, and, as the fire sank low, they began to shiver with the cold. Lucky was it for them that the Indians discovered them, else they had certainly been frozen to death that night.

Hawk roused them with little ceremony. Roy, by an impulse which would appear to be natural to those who dwell in wild countries, whether young or old, seized his axe, which lay beside him, as he leaped up. Hawk grinned, and took the axe from him at once, and the poor boy, seeing that he was surrounded by dark warriors, offered no resistance, but sought to comfort Nelly, who was clinging to him and trembling with terror.

Immediately the savages sat down in the encampment, and began an earnest discussion, which the children watched with great eagerness. They evidently did not agree, for much gesticulation and great vehemence characterised their debate. Some pointed towards the Fort, and touched their tomahawks, while others pointed to the woods in the direction whence they had come, and shook their heads. Not a few drew their scalping knives partially from their sheaths, and, pointing to the children, showed clearly that they wished to cut their career short without delay, but several of the more sedate members of the party evidently objected to this. Finally, Hawk turned to Roy, and said something to him in the Indian tongue.

Roy did not understand, and attempted to say so as well as he could by signs, and the use of the few words of the Cree language which his father had taught him. In the course of his speech (if we may use that term), he chanced to mention Wapaw's name.

"Ho! ho! ho!" said one and another of the Indians, while Hawk grinned horribly.

A variety of questions were now put to poor Roy, who, not understanding, of course could not answer them. Hawk, however, repeated Wapaw's name, and pointed towards the Fort with a look of inquiry, to which Roy replied by nodding his head and repeating "Wapaw" once or twice, also pointing to the Fort; for he began to suspect these must be Wapaw's comrades, who had come to search for him. He therefore volunteered a little additional information by means of signs; rubbed his stomach, looked dreadfully rueful, rolled himself as if in agony on the ground, and then, getting up, pretended to eat and look happy! By all of which he meant to show how that Wapaw had been on the borders of starvation, but had been happily saved therefrom.

Indians in council might teach a useful lesson to our members of parliament, for they witnessed this rather laughable species of pantomime with profound gravity and silence. When Roy concluded, they nodded their heads, and said, "Ho! ho!" which, no doubt, was equivalent to "Hear hear!"

After a little more discussion they rose to depart, and made signs to the children to get up and follow. Roy then pointed out the broken state of his snowshoe, but this difficulty was overcome by Hawk, who threw it away, and made him put on his sister's snowshoes. A stout young warrior was ordered to take Nelly on his back, which he did without delay, and the whole party left the encampment, headed by their chief.

The children submitted cheerfully at first, under the impression that the Indians meant to convey them to the Fort. Great, however, was their horror when they were taken through the woods by a way which they knew to be quite in the opposite direction.

When Roy saw this he stopped and looked back, but an Indian behind him gave him a poke with the butt of his gun which there was no resisting. For a moment the lad thought of trying to break away, run home, and tell his father of Nelly's fate; but a second thought convinced him that this course was utterly impracticable. As for Nelly, she was too far from her brother in the procession to hold converse with him; and, as she knew not what to do, say, think, she was reduced to the miserable consolation of bedewing with her tears the shoulders of the young warrior who carried her.

The storm which had commenced the day before still continued, so that, in the course of a few hours, traces of the track of the war-party were almost obliterated, and the chance of their being followed by

Robin and his friends was rendered less and less likely as time ran on.

All that day they travelled without halt, and when they stopped at night to encamp, Roy was nearly dead from exhaustion. "My poor Nell," said he, drawing his sobbing sister close to him, as they sat near the camp fire, after having eaten the small quantity of dried venison that was thrown to them by their captors, "don't despair; father will be sure to hunt us down, if it's in the power of man to do it."

"I don't despair," sobbed Nelly; "but oh! what will darling mother do when she finds that we're lost, and I'm so afraid they'll kill us."

"No fear o' that, Nell; it's not worth their while. Remember, too, what mother often told us — that — that — what is it she used to read so often out of the Bible? I forget."

"I think it was, 'Call upon Me in the time of trouble, and I will deliver thee.' I've been thinkin' of that, Roy, already."

"That's right, Nell; now, come, cheer up! Have you had enough to eat?"

"Yes," said Nelly, with a loud yawn, which she did not attempt to check.

Roy echoed it, as a matter of course, (who ever did see anyone yawn without following suit?) and then the two lay down together, spread over themselves an old blanket which one of the Indians had given them, and fell asleep at once.

Day succeeded day, night followed night, and weeks came and went, yet the Indians continued their journey through the snow-clad wilderness. Roy's snowshoes had been picked up and repaired by one of the savages, and Nelly was made to walk a good deal on her own snow-shoes; but it is justice to the Indians to say that they slackened their pace a little for the sake of the children, and when Nelly showed symptoms of being fatigued, the stout young warrior who originally carried her took her on his shoulders.

At length the encampment of the tribe was reached, and Nelly was handed over to Hawk's wife to be her slave. Soon after that the tents were struck, and the whole tribe went deeper into the northern wilds. Several gales arose and passed away, completely covering their footprints, so that no tracks were left behind them.

CHAPTER VI.

The Camp, the Attack, and the Escape.

It were vain to attempt a description of the varied condition of mind into which the brother and sister fell when they found themselves actually reduced to a state of slavery in an Indian camp, and separated from their parents, as they firmly believed, for ever.

Nelly wept her eyes almost out of their sockets at first. Then she fell into a sort of apathetic state, in which, for several days, she went about her duties almost mechanically, feeling as if it were all a horrible dream, out of which she would soon awake, and find herself at home with her "darling mother" beside her. This passed, however, and she had another fit of heart-breaking sorrow, from which she found relief by recalling some of the passages in God's Word, which her mother had taught her to repeat by heart; especially that verse in which it is said, "that Jesus is a friend who sticketh closer than a brother." And this came to the poor child's mind with peculiar power, because her own brother Roy was so kind, and took such pains to comfort her, and to enter into all her girlish feelings and sympathies, that she could scarcely imagine it possible for anyone to stick closer to her in all her distress than he did.

As for Roy, he was not given to the melting mood. His nature was bold and manly. Whatever he felt, he kept it to himself, and he forgot more than half his own sorrow in his brotherly efforts to assuage that of Nelly.

Both of them were active and willing to oblige, so that they did not allow their grief to interfere with their work, a circumstance which induced their captors to treat them with forbearance, and even kindness. Nelly sobbed and worked; gradually, the sobbing decreased, and the work was carried on with vigour, so that she soon became quite expert at skinning rabbits, boiling meat, embroidering mocassins, smoking deerskins, chopping firewood into small pieces, and many other details of Indian household economy; while Roy went out with the hunters, and became a very Nimrod, insomuch that he soon excelled all the lads of his own age, and many of those who were older, in the use of the bow, the snowshoes, the spear, the axe, and the gun. But all this, and what they did and said in the Indian camp during that winter, and what was said and done to them, we do not mean to write about, having matter of deeper interest to tell.

Winter passed away, and spring came. But little do those who dwell in England know of the enchantment of returning spring in the frozen wilderness of North America. The long, long winter, seems as though it would *never* pass away. The intense frost seals up all the sweet odours of the woods for so many months, that the nostrils become powerfully sensitive, and, as it were, yearn for something to smell. The skin gets so used to frost, that a balmy breeze is thought of as a thing of the past, or well-nigh forgotten.

Spring in those regions comes suddenly. It came on our wanderers with a gush. One night the temperature rose high above the freezing point; next day all the sights and sounds of Nature's great awakening were in full play. The air fanned their cheeks like a summer breeze; the strange unwonted sound of tinkling and dropping water was heard; scents, as of green things, were met and inhaled greedily. As the thirsty Bedouin drinks from the well in the oasis, so did Roy and Nelly drink in the delicious influences of melting nature. And they thought of those words which say, that the wilderness shall rejoice and blossom as the rose. The rejoicing had commenced, the blossoming would soon follow.

But warlike and wicked men were even then preparing to desecrate the beautiful land. A war-party of enemies had come down upon the tribe with whom they dwelt. Scouts had brought in the news. All was commotion and excitement in the camp. Goods and chattels were being packed up. The women and children were to be sent off with these, under an escort, to a place of greater security, while the Braves armed for the fight.

In the middle of all the confusion, Roy took Nelly aside, and, with a look of mystery, said —

"Nell, dear, I'm goin' to run away. Stay, now, don't stare so like an owl, but hold your sweet tongue until I have explained what I mean to do. You and I have picked up a good deal of useful knowledge of one sort or another since we came here, and I'm inclined to think we are quite fit to take to the woods and work our way back to Fort Enterprise."

"But isn't it an *awful* long way?" said Nelly.

"It is, but we have an *awful* long time to travel; haven't we all our lives before us? If our lives are long, we'll manage it; if they are short, why, we won't want to manage it, so we need not bother our heads about that?"

"But the way home," suggested Nelly, "do you know it?"

"Of course I know it; that is to say, I know, from that ugly thief Hawk, that it lies somewhere or other to the south-west o' this place, some hundreds of miles off; how many hundreds does not much matter, for we have got the whole of the spring, summer, and fall before us."

"But what if we don't get home in the fall?"

"Then we shall spend the winter in the woods, that's all."

Nelly laughed, in spite of her anxieties, at the confident tone in which her brother spoke; and, being quite unable to argue the matter farther, she said that she was ready to do whatever Roy pleased, having perfect confidence in his wisdom.

"That's right, Nell; now, you get ready to start at a moment's notice. When the Injuns attack the camp, we'll give 'em the slip. Put all you want to take with you on a toboggan,[1] and meet me at the crooked tree when the camp moves."

That night the camp was struck, and the women and children departed, under a strong escort. Almost at the same time the enemy came down on their prey, but they met men prepared for them. In the dark, Nelly crept to the crooked tree, dragging the toboggan after her. She was met by Roy, who took the sledge-line and her hand and led her into the dark forest, while the savages were fighting and yelling like

---

1   A small Indian sledge, dragged on the snow, either by hand or by dog with loops at the sides for lashing the loading of the sledge upon it.

fiends in the camp. There let us leave them to fight it out. Enough for us to know that their warfare prevented any pursuit of the young fugitives.

Weeks passed, and Roy and Nelly wandered on; all fear of pursuit soon left them. Ducks, geese, and other waterfowl, came in myriads with the spring. Roy had brought with him his gun (the one he was wont to use in hunting), and bow and quiver. They fed on the fat of the land. Summer advanced, and game became less plentiful; still, there was more than sufficient to supply them with abundance of food. Autumn approached; the wild fowl that had passed northward in spring, began to return southward, and again the wants of the young wanderers were superabundantly supplied.

The pole-star was Roy's guide. At night he laid his course by it; and by the sun during the day, making constant allowance, of course, for the sun's rate of travelling through the sky, and taking advantage of all prominent landmarks on the way.

Time sped on; many weary miles were travelled, but no sign of Fort Enterprise was to be seen. Day after day, week after week, month after month they wandered, and still found themselves in the heart of an unknown wilderness. Occasionally they observed signs of Indians, and carefully kept out of sight at such times, as you may easily believe.

At last there came a day when hard frost set in. It was the first touch of another winter. Roy and Nelly did not betray their feelings to each other, but their hearts sank as they thought of what lay before them. The frost was short-lived, however; towards noon the air became delightfully warm, and their spirits revived.

On reaching the summit of an eminence, up which they had toiled for several hours, they beheld a small lake, in which the silvery clouds were clearly reflected. The day was calm; the sun unusually brilliant; the autumnal foliage most gorgeous in colour. It was like a scene in fairy-land!

"Splendid!" exclaimed Roy, sitting down beside his sister on the trunk of a fallen tree.

"Oh! *how* beautiful," cried Nelly.

"It's so like silver," said Roy.

"Silver Lake," murmured Nelly.

Roy seemed to think the name appropriate, for he echoed the words, "Yes, Silver Lake." And there brother and sister sat, for a long time, on the fallen tree, in silent admiration of the scene.

CHAPTER VII.

The Encampment on Silver Lake.

When Roy and Nelly sat down to gaze in admiration on Silver Lake, they little thought how long a period they should have to spend on its shores.

The lake was a small sheet of water not more than half a mile broad, embosomed among low hills, which, though not grand, were picturesque in outline, and wooded to their tops. It occupied the summit of an elevated region or height-of-land — a water-shed, in fact — and Roy afterwards discovered that water flowed from both the north-east and south-west sides of the table-land, in the midst of which it lay. These fountain-heads, separated by little more than half a mile from each other, were the sources of streams, which, flowing in opposite directions through hundreds of miles of wild, beautiful, and uncultivated wilderness, found their way, on the one hand, into Hudson's Bay, on the other hand, into the Atlantic through the great rivers and lakes of Canada.

The waters of the lake were strikingly clear and pellucid. When the young wanderer first came upon the scene, not a zephyr stirred the leaves of the forest; the blue sky was studded with towering masses of white clouds which glowed in sunshine, and these reflected in the glassy water — as if far, far down in its unfathomable depths — produced that silvery effect which prompted Nelly to utter the name which we have adopted.

Small though the Silver Lake was, it boasted two islets, which like twin babes lay side by side on their mother's fair breast, their reflected images stretching down into that breast as if striving to reach and grasp its heart!

"Couldn't we stay here a short time?" asked Nelly, breaking the silence in a tone that indicated anxiety, hope, and enthusiasm, "only for a very *little* time," she added, coaxingly.

Roy looked grave and sagacious. Boys as well as men like to be leant upon and trusted by the fair sex — at least in things masculine — and Nelly had such boundless faith in her brother's capacity to protect her and guide her through the forest, that she unwittingly inspired him with an exuberant amount of courage and self-reliance. The lad was bold and fearless enough by nature. His sister's confidence in him had the effect of inducing him to think himself fit for anything! He affected, therefore, at times, a look of grave sagacity, befitting, as he thought, so important and responsible a character.

"I've just been thinking," said he.

"Oh! don't *think*, but say yes!" interrupted Nelly.

"Well, I'm going to say yes, but I meant to give you my reasons for sayin' so. In the first place, my powder and shot is gettin' low. You see I did not bring away very much from the Injun camp, and we've been using it for so many months now that it won't last much longer, so I think it would not be a bad plan to stop here awhile and fish and shoot and feed up — for you need rest, Nelly — and then start fresh with a well-loaded sledge. I'll save some powder by using the bow we made the other day."

"But you forget it's broken."

"So it is — never mind, we can make another — there's a tree that will make a first-rater down in the hollow, d'ye see it, Nell?"

"Where — oh yes — just by the grassy place where the rock juts out into the water with the sun shining on it? what a *nice* place to build a hut!"

"Just so," said Roy, smiling at the girl's enthusiasm, "that's the spot, and that's the very thought that jumped bang into my brain as you spoke. By the way, does a thought jump *into* a man's brain or *out* of it, I wonder?"

"Out of it, of course," cried Nelly, with a laugh.

"I'm not so sure of that, Nell. I send it rather slowly out through my mouth, but I think it jumps *into* my brain. I wonder how it gets in; whether by the eyes, or ears, or mouth — perhaps it goes up the nose."

"What stuff you do talk!" cried Nelly.

"D'ye think so," said Roy with a grin, "well, that bein' the case, let's go and fix our camp, for the sun is not given to sitting up all night in these parts, so we must work while it shines."

With hurried steps and eager looks, (for Roy, despite his affected coolness, was as enthusiastic about the new plan as his sister,) they descended to the margin of Silver Lake, and began to make their encampment on the sunny spot before referred to.

It turned out to be most suitable for their purpose, having a gentle slope towards the margin of the lake, which was fringed with a beach of pure white pebbles, and being well sheltered in the rear by umbrageous trees. The point of rocks close at hand formed a natural jetty, which, Roy observed, would be useful as a landing-place when he got his raft under way; the turf was soft, a matter of some importance, as it was to form their couch at night, and a small stream trickled down from one of the numerous springs which welled up at the foot of the nearest hill.

Solitary and remote from the usual haunts of men as this lake was, there was no feeling of solitude about it at the time we write of. The entire region was alive with wild fowl of many kinds. Wild geese trumpeted their advent as they came from the far north, *en route* for the far south, and settled on the bosom of Silver Lake to take a night's lodging there. Ducks, from the same region, and bound for the same goal — though with less stately and regular flight — flew hither and thither with whistling wings, ever and anon going swash into the water as a tempting patch of reeds invited them to feed, or a whim of fancy induced them to rest. Wild swans occasionally sailed in all their majesty on its waters, while plover of every length of limb and bill, and every species of plaintive cry, waded round its margin, or swept in clouds over the neighbouring swamps. Sometimes deer would trot out of the woods and slake their thirst on its shore, and the frequent rings that broke its smooth surface told of life in the watery depths below.

The whole air was filled with gushing sounds of wild melody, as though bird and beast were uniting in a hymn of praise to the beneficent Creator who had provided the means of, and given the capacity for, so much enjoyment.

Having decided on a suitable spot for their temporary resting-place, Roy's first care was to construct a hut. This was neither a work of time nor difficulty. In a couple of hours it was finished. He commenced the work by felling about a dozen young fir-trees not much thicker than a man's wrist, from which he chopped the branches, thus leaving them bare poles about nine feet long. While he was thus employed, his sister cleared the spot on which their dwelling was to stand, and, having an eye to the picturesque, so arranged that the opening of the hut should command an uninterrupted view of the lake. On going into the "bush" to the place where Roy was at work, she found him cutting down his sixth tree, and the ground was strewn with the flat branches of those already cut.

"Come along, Nelly – how hot I am – carry these branches into camp, lass, an' go ahead, for I've got supper to kill yet."

Nelly made no direct reply, but muttered to herself something that sounded very like, "Oh, what fun!" as she filled her tiny arms with pine branches, and, hugging them to her heaving breast, staggered to the camp. When she had carried all the branches, Roy had cut all the poles, so he proceeded to set them up. Tying three poles together at the top, and using the pliant roots of a tree for the purpose, he set them up in the form of a tripod. Against these three all the other poles were piled, crossing each other at the top, and spreading out at the base so as to enclose a circle of about six feet in diameter. Being numerous, the poles were pretty close together, thus affording good support to the branches which were afterwards piled on them. Pine branches are flat, spreading, and thick, so that when laid above each other to a depth of several inches they form a very good shelter from dew and light rain. The hut was entirely covered with such branches, which were kept in their places by other poles leaning upon and pressing them down. The floor of the hut was also covered with pine "brush."

"Now for supper, Nelly," said Roy, seizing his bow, when the hut was completed, and splicing its broken part with a strip of deerskin cut from the lines of the sledge.

"Get a goose, Roy, and pick out a nice fat one," cried Nelly, laughing, "I'll have the fire ready when you come back."

"I'll try," said Roy, and he did try, but tried in vain. Although a good shot, he was not sufficiently expert with the bow to shoot wild fowl on the wing, so he returned to the hut empty-handed.

"We must make a new bow, Nell," said he, sitting down by the fire, "I can do nothin' wi' this, and it won't do to use the gun for anythin' but deer. Meanwhile let's have the remains of our dinner for supper. Come, cheer up, old 'ooman; we shall feast on the fat of the land tomorrow!"

The stars were shining in the sky, and winking at their reflections down in the depths of Silver Lake, and the lake itself lay, as black as ink, under the shadow of the hills, when the brother and sister spread their blanket above them that night, and sank, almost immediately, into profound slumber.

CHAPTER VIII.

Hunting, and other Matters, on Silver Lake.

Sunrise is a gladsome event almost at all times; we say "almost," because there are times when sunrise is *not* particularly gladsome. In the arctic regions of Norway, for instance, we have seen it rise only twenty minutes after it set, and the rising and setting were so much mingled, that no very strong feelings of any kind were awakened. Moreover, we were somewhat depressed at the time, in consequence of having failed to reach those latitudes where the sun does not set at all for several weeks in summer, but shines night and day. To the sick, sunrise brings little comfort; too often it is watched for with weariness, and beheld, at last, with a feeling of depression at the thought that another day of pain has begun. But to the healthy, and especially to the young, sunrise is undoubtedly, on most occasions, a gladsome event.

At least Nelly Gore thought so when she awoke and beheld, from the floor of the hut where she lay, a flood of yellow glory gushing through a valley, turning Silver Lake into gold, tipping the trees with fire, and blazing full in Roy's face, which was at that moment turned up to the sky with the mouth open, and the nose snoring.

"Oh, *how* beautiful!" screamed Nelly, in the exuberance of her delight.

"Hallo! murder! come on, ye black varmints," shouted Roy, as he sprang up and seized the axe which lay at his side. "Oh, it's only *you*, what a yell you do give, Nelly! why, one would think you were a born Injun; what is't all about, lass? Ye-a-ow! how sleepy I am — too late to have another nap, I suppose, eh?"

"Oh yes, lazy thing! get up and come out quick!" cried the other, as she sprang up and ran out of the hut to enjoy the full blaze of the sunshine, and the fresh morning air.

That morning Nelly could do little but ramble about in a wild sort of fashion, trying to imagine that she was queen of the world around her! She sobered down, however, towards noon, and went diligently about the work which Roy had given her to do. She had the internal arrangements of the hut to complete and improve, some pairs of mocassins to mend, and several arrows to feather, besides other matters.

Meanwhile Roy went out to hunt.

Determined not to use his fast-diminishing ammunition, except on large game, and anxious to become more expert with the bow, he set to work the first thing that day, and made a new bow. Armed with this and a dozen arrows, he sallied forth.

Some of his arrows were pointed with ivory, some with iron, and some had no points at all, but blunt heavy heads instead. These latter were, and still are, used by Indians in shooting game that is tame and easily killed. Grouse of various kinds, for instance, if hit with full force from a short range by a blunt-headed arrow, will be effectually stunned, especially if hit on the head.

At first Roy walked along the shores of the lake, but was not very successful, because the ducks and geese were hid among reeds, and rose suddenly with a distracting *whirr*, usually flying off over the water. To have let fly at these would have cost him an arrow every shot, so, after losing one, he wisely restrained himself.

After a time, he turned into the woods, resolving to try his fortune where his arrows were not so likely to be lost. He had not gone far, when a tree-grouse sprang into the air and settled on a neighbouring pine.

Roy became excited, for he was anxious not to return to the hut empty-handed a second time. He fitted a sharp-headed arrow to the string, and advanced towards the bird cautiously. His anxiety to make little noise was so great, that he tripped over a root and fell with a hideous crash into the middle of a dead bush, the branches of which snapped like a discharge of little crackers. Poor Roy got up disgusted, but on looking up found that the grouse was still sitting there, filled apparently with more curiosity than alarm. Seeing this he advanced to within a few yards of the bird, and, substituting a blunt arrow for the sharp one, discharged it with vigour. It hit the grouse on the left eye, and brought it to the ground like a stone.

"Good, that's 'number one,'" muttered the lad as he fastened the bird to his belt; "hope 'number two' is not far off."

"Number two" was nearer than he imagined, for four other birds of the same kind rose a few yards ahead of him, with all the noise and flurry that is characteristic of the species.

They settled on a tree not far off, and looked about them.

"Sit there, my fine fellows, till I come up," muttered Roy. (The lad had a habit of speaking to himself while out hunting.)

They obeyed the order, and sat until he was close to them. Again was the blunt arrow fitted to the string; once more it sped true to its mark, and "number two" fell fluttering to the ground.

Now, the grouse of North America is sometimes a very stupid creature. It literally sits still to be shot, if the hunter is only careful to fire first at the lowest bird of the group. If he were to fire at the topmost one, its fluttering down amongst the others would start them off.

Roy was aware of this fact, and had aimed at the bird that sat lowest on the tree. Another arrow was discharged, and "number three" lay sprawling on the ground. The blunt arrows being exhausted, he now tried a sharp one, but missed. The birds stretched their necks, turned their heads on one side, and looked at the lad, as though to say, "It won't do, — try again!"

Another shaft was more successful. It pierced the heart of "number four," and brought it down like a lump of lead. "Number five" seemed a little perplexed by this time, and made a motion as though it were about to fly off, but an arrow caught it in the throat, and cut short its intentions and its career. Thus did Roy bag, or rather belt, five birds consecutively.[2]

Our hero was not one of those civilised sportsmen who slaughter as much game as they can. He merely wanted to provide food for a day or two. He therefore turned his steps homeward — if we may be allowed the expression — being anxious to assist his sister in making the hut comfortable.

As he walked along, his active mind ran riot in many eccentric

2   The author has himself, in the backwoods, taken four birds in succession off a tree in this fashion with a fowling-piece.

channels. Those who take any interest in the study of mind, know that it is not only the mind of a romantic boy that does this, but that the mind of man generally is, when left to itself, the veriest acrobat, the most unaccountable harlequin, that ever leaped across the stage of fancy.

Roy's mind was now in the clouds, now on the earth. Anon it was away in the far-off wilderness, or scampering through the settlements, and presently it was deep down in Silver Lake playing with the fish. Roy himself muttered a word or so, now and then, as he walked along, which gave indication of the whereabouts of his mind at the time.

"Capital fun," said he, "only it won't do to stay too long. Poor mother, how she'll be wearin' for us! Hallo! ducks, you're noisy coons, wonder why you get up with such a bang. Bang! that reminds me of the gun. No more banging of you, old chap, if my hand keeps in so well with the bow. Eh! duck, what's wrong?"

This latter question was addressed to a small duck which seemed in an anxious state of mind, to judge from its motions. Presently a head, as if of a fish, broke the surface of the lake, and the duck disappeared!

"Oh the villain," exclaimed Roy, "a fish has bolted him!"

After this the lad walked on in silence, looking at the ground, and evidently pondering deeply.

"Nelly," said he, entering the hut and throwing the grouse at her feet, "here is dinner, supper, and breakfast for you, and please get the first ready as fast as you can, for I'm famishing."

"Oh, how nice! how did you get them?"

"I'll tell you presently, but my head's full of a notion about catching ducks just now."

"Catching ducks, Roy, what is the notion?"

"Never mind, Nelly, I han't scratched it out o' my brain yet, but I'll tell 'ee after dinner, and we'll try the plan tomorrow mornin'."

CHAPTER IX.

Fishing Extraordinary.

Early on the following morning, Roy and Nelly rose to try the new style of duck-hunting which the former had devised.

"I wonder if it will do," said the little girl, as she tripped along by her brother's side in the direction of a marshy bay, which had been selected as the scene of their experiments. "How clever of you to invent such a funny plan!"

"Well, I didn't exactly invent it, lass. The fact is, that I remembered father havin' told me he had read it in a book before he left the settlements. I *wish* we had some books. Pity that we've got no books."

"So it is," assented Nell, with a touch of sadness in her tone.

Both Roy and his sister were good readers, having been taught by their mother out of the Bible — the only book that Robin Gore had brought with him from the settlements. Robin could read, but he did not care much for reading — neither did Walter nor Larry O'Dowd. Indeed the latter could not read at all. Mrs. Gore had wanted to take a few books with her into the wilderness, but her husband said he thought the Bible was enough for her; so the library at Fort Enterprise was select and small! One good resulted from this — the Bible was read, by all who could read, a great deal more than would have been the case had there been other books at hand. But the young people longed earnestly for books containing fairy tales, such as was told to them by their mother; and wild adventures, such as Walter could relate or invent by the hour.

It might have been observed that Roy carried on his shoulder a remarkable object — something like a clumsy basket made of reeds, and about twice the size of a man's head. This had been made by Nelly the night before. The use to which it was to be put was soon shown by Roy. Having reached the spot where the experiment was to be tried, and having observed that there were many ducks, large and small, floating about among the reeds, he got Nelly to hold the basket, if we may so call it, as high as she could raise it. There was a hole in the bottom of it.

Through this Roy thrust his head, so that the machine rested on his shoulders, his head being inside and completely concealed.

"Now, Nelly, what think you of my helmet?"

"Oh! it is splendid!" cried the girl, laughing in a subdued voice. "It's so awfully absurd looking, but can you see? for I don't see a bit of your face."

"See? ay, as well as need be. There's lots of small holes which I can peep through in all directions. But come, I'll try it. Keep close, Nell, and don't laugh too loud, for ducks ain't used to laughing, d'ye see, and may be frightened by it."

So saying Roy crept on his hands and knees to the edge of the lake, being concealed by bushes, until he got into the water. Here a few steps took him into the reeds which clustered so thickly at that spot, and grew so tall that he was soon hidden from sight altogether.

He had not taken off much of his dress, which, we may remark in passing, was of the simplest at all times — consisting of a pair of trousers, a striped cotton shirt, and a grey cloth capote with a hood to it. His capote and cap were left in charge of his sister. As for the shirt and trousers, they could be easily dried again.

Nelly watched the place where her brother had disappeared with breathless interest. As he did not reappear as quickly as she had expected, she became greatly alarmed. In a few minutes more she would certainly have rushed into the lake to the rescue, regardless of consequences and of ducks, had not Roy's strange headdress come suddenly into view at the outward verge of the reeds. The lad had waded in up to his neck, and was now slowly — almost imperceptibly — approaching a group of ducks that were disporting themselves gaily in the water.

"They'll never let him near them," thought Nelly.

She was wrong, for at that moment an extremely fat and pert young duck observed the bundle of reeds, and swam straight up to it, animated, no doubt, by that reckless curiosity which is peculiar to young creatures. Had its mother known what was inside of the bundle, she would no doubt have remonstrated with her headstrong child, but, old and sagacious though that mother was, she was completely deceived. She was not even astonished when her duckling suddenly disappeared beneath the water, thinking, no doubt, that it had dived. Soon the bundle of reeds drew near to the mother, and she, too, disappeared suddenly below the water. Whatever her astonishment was at feeling her legs seized from below, she had not time to express it before her voice was choked. Nelly observed these disappearances with intense amazement, and delight stamped every lineament of her little visage.

When the bundle moved towards the father of the duck-family, that gentleman became agitated and suspicious. Probably males are less trusting than females, in all conditions of animal life. At all events he sheered off. The bundle waxed impatient and made a rush at him. The drake, missing his wife and child, quacked the alarm. The bundle made another rush, and suddenly disappeared with a tremendous splash, in the midst of which a leg and an arm appeared! Away went the whole brood of ducks with immense splutter, and Nelly gave a wild scream of terror, supposing — and she was right — that her brother had fallen into a hole, and that he would be drowned. In the latter supposition, however, she was mistaken, for Roy swam ashore in a few moments with a duck in each hand!

"O Roy! ain't you cold?" inquired Nelly, as she helped him to squeeze the water out of his garments.

"Y–y–ye-es," said Roy, trembling in every limb, while his teeth rattled like small castanets, "I'm very c–c–c-cold, but I'm in luck, for I've g–g–g-got tonight's s–s–s-supper, anyhow."

This was true, but as he could not hope to procure many more suppers in the same fashion at that season of the year, he and his sister went off without delay to try the fishing.

They had brought a fishing line and a few hooks, among other small things, from the Indian camp. This line was now got out, overhauled, and baited with a bit of the young duck's breast. From the end of the point of rocks, which had been named the Wharf, the line was cast, for there the lake was deep.

"Take the end of the line, Nell; I want you to catch the first fish."

"How d'ye know we shall catch — oh! oh — ooh!" The fish in Silver Lake had never seen a bait or felt a hook in their lives before that day. They actually fought for the prize. A big bully — as is usually the case in other spheres of life — gained it, and found he had "caught a Tartar." He nearly pulled Nelly into the lake, but Roy sprang to the rescue, and before the child's shout of surprise had ceased to echo among the cliffs, a beautiful silvery fish, about a foot and a half long, lay tumbling on the strand.

"Hurray!" cried Roy. "Try again."

They did try again, and again, and over again, until they had caught two dozen and a half of those peculiar "white-fish" which swarm in most of the lakes of North America. Then they stopped, being somewhat exhausted, and having more than enough for present use.

Before sitting down to supper that night, they preserved their fish in the simple but effective manner which is practised among the fur-traders in cold weather, and which they had learned while with the Indians. Each fish was split open and cleaned out, and then hung up by the tail to dry.

"What a jolly time we shall have of it!" said Roy, with his mouth full, as he sat beside Nelly and toasted his toes that night at supper.

"Yes," said Nelly — "if — if we were only a *little* nearer home."

This reply made them both silent and sad for a time.

"Never mind," resumed Roy, cheerily, as he began another white-fish — having already finished one fish and the duckling — "cheer up, Nell, we'll stay here long enough to get up a stock o' dried meat, and then set off again. I only wish it would come frost, to make our fish keep."

Roy's wish was gratified sooner than he expected, and much more fully than he desired.

CHAPTER X.

Changes, Sliding, Fishing, Etc.

That night King Frost spread his wings over the land with unwonted suddenness and rigour, insomuch that a sheet of ice, full an inch thick, sealed up the waters of Silver Lake.

Roy and Nelly had feasted heartily, and had piled wood on the fire so high that the hut was comparatively warm, and they slept soundly till morning: but, about sunrise, the fire having died out, they both awoke shivering with cold. Being *very* sleepy, they tried for some time to drop off again in spite of the cold. Failing in this, Roy at last jumped up with vigour and said he would light the fire, but he had scarcely issued from the hut, when a shout brought Nelly in alarm and haste to his side.

If Silver Lake was worthy of its name before, it was infinitely more worthy of it now. The sun had just overtopped the opposite ridge, and was streaming over a very world of silver. The frozen lake was like a sheet of the purest glass, which reflected the silvery clouds and white rolling mists of morning as perfectly in their form as the realities that floated in the blue sky. Every tree, every twig, seemed made of silver, being encased in hoar-frost, and as these moved very gently in the calm air — for there was no breeze — millions of crystalline points caught the sun's rays and scattered them around with dazzling lustre. Nature seemed robed in cloth of diamonds; but the comparison is feeble, for what diamonds, cut by man, can equal those countless crystal gems that are fashioned by the hand of God to decorate, for an hour or two, the spotless robe of a winter morning?

Had Roy been a man and Nelly a woman, the two would probably have cast around a lingering glance of admiration, and then gone quietly about their avocations; but, being children, they made up their minds, on the spot, to enjoy the state of things to the utmost. They ran down to the lake and tried the ice. Finding that it was strong enough to bear them, they advanced cautiously out upon its glassy surface; then they tried to slide, but did not succeed well, owing to their soft mocassins being ill adapted for sliding. Then they picked up stones, and tried how far they could make them skim out on the lake.

"How I wish we could slide!" exclaimed Nelly, pausing in the midst of her amusement.

Roy also paused, and appeared to meditate for a minute.

"So you shall," said he quickly. "Come and let us breakfast, and I'll make you a pair of sliders."

"Sliders! what are they?"

"You shall see; get breakfast ready, a man's fit for nothing without grub."

While breakfast was preparing, Roy began to fashion wooden soles for his sister's feet and his own. These he fixed on by means of strips of deerskin, which were sunk into grooves in the under part of the soles to prevent them from chafing. Rough and ready they were, nevertheless they fitted well and tightly to their feet; but it was found that the want of a joint at the instep rendered it difficult to walk with these soles on, and impossible to run. Roy's ingenuity, however, soon overcame this difficulty. He cut the soles through just under the instep, and then, boring two holes in each part, lashed them firmly together with deerskin, thus producing a joint or hinge. Eager to try this new invention, he fastened on his own "sliders" first, and, running down to the lake, made a rush at the ice and sent himself off with all his force. Never was boy more taken by surprise; he went skimming over the surface like a stone from a sling. The other side of the lake seemed to be the only termination of his journey. "What if it should not be bearing in the middle!" His delight was evinced by a cheer. It was echoed, with the addition of a laugh by Nell, who stood in rapt admiration on the shore. Roy began well, with his legs far apart and his arms in the air; then he turned round and advanced the wrong way, then he staggered — tried to recover himself; failed, shouted, cheered again, and fell flat on his back, and performed the remainder of the journey in that position!

It was a magnificent slide, and was repeated and continued, with every possible and conceivable modification, for full two hours, at the end of which time Nelly said she couldn't take another slide to save her life, and Roy felt as if every bone in his body were going out of joint.

"This is all very well," said Roy, as they went up to the hut together, "but it won't do much in the way of getting us a supply of meat or fish."

"That's true," assented Nelly.

"Well, then," continued Roy, "we'll rest a bit, and then set to work. It's quite plain that we can have no more wading after ducks, but the fish won't object to feed in cold weather, so we'll try them again after having had a bit to eat."

In pursuance of this plan the two went to the wharf, after having refreshed themselves, and set to work with the fishing line. Nelly baited the hook, and Roy cut a hole in the ice with his axe. Having put in the hook, and let it down to the bottom, they stood at the edge of the hole – expectant!

"Frost seems to spoil their appetite," said Roy, in a tone of disappointment, after about five minutes had elapsed.

A fish seemed to have been listening, for before Nelly could reply, there came a violent tug at the line. Roy returned a still more violent tug, and, instead of hauling it up hand over hand, ran swiftly along the ice, drawing the line after him, until the fish came out of the hole with a flop and a severe splutter. It was above four pounds weight, and they afterwards found that the deeper the water into which the line was cast the larger were the fish procured. White-fish were the kind they caught most of, but there were a species of trout, much resembling a salmon in colour and flavour, of which they caught a good many above ten and even fifteen pounds weight. All these fish, except those reserved for immediate use, they cleaned and hung up in the manner already described.

Thus they occupied themselves for several days, and as the work was hard, they did not wander much from their hut, but ate their meals with appetite, and slept at nights soundly.

One night, just as they were about to lay down to rest, Roy went out to fetch an armful of firewood. He returned with a look of satisfaction on his face.

"Look here, Nell, what call ye that?" pointing to a few specks of white on his breast and arms.

"Snow!" exclaimed Nelly.

"Ay — snow! it's come at last, and I am glad of it, for we have far more than enough o' grub now, and it's time we were off from this. You see, lass, we can't expect to find much game on a journey in winter, so we must carry all we can with us. Our backs won't take so much as the sled, but the sled can't go loaded till there's snow on the ground, so the moment there is enough of it we'll set off. Before starting, hows'ever, I must go off and try for a deer, for men can't walk well on fish alone; and when I'm away you can be getting the snowshoes repaired, and the sled-lashings overhauled. We will set about all that tomorrow."

"But isn't tomorrow Sabbath?" said Nelly.

"So 'tis! I forgot; well, we can put it off till Monday."

It may be well here to remark that Mrs. Gore, being a sincere Christian, had a great reverence for the Sabbath-day, and had imbued her children with some of her own spirit in regard to it.

During the troubles and anxieties of the period when the children were lost in the snow and captured by the Indians, they had lost count of the days of the week. Roy was not much troubled about this, but his sister's tender conscience caused her much uneasiness; and when they afterwards ran away from the Indians, and could do as they pleased, they agreed together to fix a Sabbath-day for themselves, beginning with the particular day on which it first occurred to them that they had not kept a Sabbath "for a long, long time."

"We can't find out the right day now, you know," observed Nelly, in an apologetic tone.

"Of course not," said Roy; "besides, it don't matter, because you remember how it is in the Ten Commandments: 'Six days shalt thou labour and do all thy work, but the *seventh* day is the Sabbath.' We will keep *today*, then; work *six* days, and then keep the *seventh* day."

We have elsewhere observed that Roy was a bit of a philosopher. Having reasoned the matter out thus philosophically, the children held to their resolve; they travelled six days, and observed every seventh day as the Sabbath.

The particular Sabbath-day about which we are writing turned out to be a memorable one, as we shall see.

Roy and Nelly lay down that night, side by side, as was their wont, with their separate blankets wrapped around them, and their feet pointing towards the fire. Of course they never undressed at night on this journey, but washed their underclothing as they found time and opportunity.

Soon they were sound asleep, and their gentle breathing was the only sound that broke the stillness of the night. But snow was falling silently in thick heavy flakes, and it soon lay deep on the bosom of Silver Lake. Towards morning the wind arose, and snow-drift began to whirl round the hut, and block up its low doorway.

Still the brother and sister slumbered peacefully, undisturbed by the gathering storm.

CHAPTER XI.

A Change in the Weather — Rabbits and Bears Appear.

"Hi! Hallo! I say, Nelly, what's all this?" There was good cause for the tone of surprise in which Roy uttered these words when he awoke, for the fireplace and the lower half of his own, as well as his sister's, blanket were covered with at least half a foot of snow. It had found its way in at the hole in the roof of the hut, and the wind had blown a great deal through the crevices of the doorway, so that a snow-wreath more than a foot high lay close to Nelly's elbow.

This was bad enough, but what made it worse was that a perfect hurricane was blowing outside. Fortunately the hut was sheltered by the woods, and by a high cliff on the windward side; but this cliff, although it broke the force of the gale, occasioned an eddy which sent fearful gusts and thick clouds of snow ever and anon full against the doorway.

"O Roy! what shall we do?" said Nelly, in an anxious tone.

"Don't know," said Roy, jumping up and tightening his belt; "you never can know what's got to be done till you've took an observation o' what's goin' on, as daddy used to say. Hallo! hold on. I say, if it goes on like this it'll blow the hut down. Come, Nelly, don't whimper; it's only a puff, after all, an' if it did capsize us, it wouldn't be the first time we had a tumble in the snow. Seems to me that we're goin' to have a stormy Sabbath, though. Rouse up, lass, and while you're clearin' off the snow, I'll go get a bundle o' sticks, and light the fire."

Roy stooped to pass under the low doorway, or, rather, hole of the hut, and bending his head to the blast passed out; while Nelly, whose heart was cheered by her brother's confident tone more than by his words, set about shovelling away the snow-drift with great activity.

Presently Roy returned, staggering under a heavy load of firewood.

"Ho! Nell," he cried, flinging down the wood with a clatter, "just you come an' see Silver Lake. Such a sight it is you never saw; but come slick off — never mind your belt; just roll your blanket round you, over head and ears — there," said he, assisting to fasten the rough garment, and seizing his sister's hand, "hold on tight by me."

"Oh, *what* a storm!" gasped the little girl, as she staggered out and came within the full force of the gale.

It was indeed a storm, such as would have appalled the hearts of youngsters less accustomed to the woods than were our hero and heroine. But Roy and Nelly had been born and bred in the midst of stormy backwoods' elements, and were not easily alarmed, chiefly because they had become accustomed to estimate correctly the extent of most of the dangers that menaced them from time to time. A gale of the fiercest kind was blowing. In its passage it bent the trees until they groaned and creaked again; it tore off the smaller twigs and whisked them up into the air; it lifted the snow in masses out of the open spots in the woods, and hurled them in cloudlike volumes everywhere; and it roared and shrieked through the valleys and round the mountain tops as if a thousand evil spirits were let loose upon the scene.

Silver Lake was still silvery in its aspect, for the white drift was flying across it like the waves of a raging sea; but here, being exposed, the turmoil was so tremendous that there was no distinguishing between earth, lake, and sky. "Confusion, worse confounded" reigned every where, or rather, appeared to reign; for, in point of fact, *there is no confusion whatever* in the works and ways of God. Common sense, if unfallen, would tell us that. The Word reveals it, and science of late years has added its testimony thereto.

Roy and Nelly very naturally came to the conclusion that things were in a very disordered state indeed on that Sabbath morning, so they returned to their hut, to spend the day as best they might.

Their first care was to kindle the fire and prepare breakfast. While Nelly was engaged in this, Roy went out and cut several small trees, with which he propped the hut all round to prevent it from being blown down. But it was discovered, first, that the fire would hardly kindle, and, second, that when it was kindled it filled the whole place with smoke. By dint of perseverance, however, breakfast was cooked and devoured, after which the fire was allowed to go out, as the smoke had almost blinded them.

"Never mind, Nell, cheer up," said Roy, on concluding breakfast; "we'll rig up a tent to keep the snow off us."

The snow, be it understood, had been falling into the fire, and, more or less, upon themselves, through the hole in the roof; so they made a tent inside the hut, by erecting two posts with a ridge-pole at a height of three feet from the ground, over which they spread one of their blankets. Under this tent they reclined with the other blankets spread over them, and chatted comfortably during the greater part of that day.

Of course their talk was chiefly of home, and of the mother who had been the sun and the joy of their existence up to that sad day when they were lost in the snow, and naturally they conversed of the Bible, and the hymns which their mother had made the chief objects of their contemplation on the Sabbaths they had spent at Fort Enterprise.

Monday was as bad as Sunday in regard to weather, but Tuesday dawned bright and calm, so that our wanderers were enabled to resume their avocations. The snowshoes were put in order, the sled was overhauled and mended, and more fish were caught and hung up to dry. In the evening Roy loaded his gun with ball, put on his snowshoes, and sallied forth alone to search for deer. He carried with him several small pieces of line wherewith to make rabbit snares; for, the moment the snow fell, innumerable tracks revealed the fact that there were thousands of rabbits in that region. Nelly, meanwhile, busied herself in putting the hut in order, and in repairing the mocassins which would be required for the journey home.

Lest any reader should wonder where our heroine found materials for all the mending and repairing referred to, we may remark that the Indians in the wilderness were, and still are, supplied with needles, beads, cloth, powder and shot, guns, axes, &c., &c., by the adventurous fur-traders, who penetrate deep and far into the wilderness of North America; and when Nelly and Roy ran away from their captors they took care to carry with them an ample supply of such things as they might require in their flight.

About half a mile from the hut Roy set several snares. He had often helped his father in such work, and knew exactly how to do it. Selecting a rabbit-track at a spot where it passed between two bushes, he set his snare so that it presented a loop in the centre of the path. This loop was fastened to the bough of a tree bent downwards, and so arranged that it held fast to a root in the ground; when a rabbit should endeavour to leap or force through it, he would necessarily pull away the fastening that held it down, and the bough would spring up and lift the hapless creature by the neck off the ground.

Having set half-a-dozen such snares, Roy continued his march in search of deer-tracks. He was unsuccessful, but to his surprise he came suddenly on the huge track of a bear! Being early in the season this particular bruin had not yet settled himself into his winter quarters, so Roy determined to make a trap for him. He had not much hope of catching him, but resolved to try, and not to tell Nelly of his discovery until he should see the result.

Against the face of a cliff he raised several huge stones so as to form a sort of box, or cave, or hole, the front of which was open, the sides being the stones referred to, and the back the cliff. Then he felled a tree as thick as his waist, which stood close by, and so managed that it fell near to his trap. By great exertions, and with the aid of a wooden lever prepared on the spot, he rolled this tree — when denuded of its branches — close to the mouth of the trap. Next he cut three small pieces of stick in such a form that they made a trigger — something like the figure 4 — on which the tree might rest. On the top of this trigger he raised the tree-stem, and on the end of the trigger, which projected into the trap, he stuck a piece of dried fish, so that when the bear should creep under the stem and touch the bait, it would disarrange the trigger, set it off, and the heavy stem would fall on bruin's back. As he knew, however, that bears were very strong, he cut several other thick stems, and piled them on the first to give it additional weight.

All being ready, and the evening far advanced, he returned to the hut to supper.

CHAPTER XII.

Roy's Dream.

"Nelly, ye-a-a-ow!" exclaimed Roy, yawning as he awoke on the following morning from a dream in which bears figured largely; "what a night I've had of it, to be sure — fightin' like a mad buffalo with —" Here Roy paused abruptly.

"Well, what were you fighting with?" asked Nell, with a smile that ended in a yawn.

"I won't tell you just now, lass, as it might spoil your appetite for breakfast. Set about getting that ready as fast as you can, for I want to be off as soon as possible to visit my snares."

"I guess we shall have rabbits for dinner today."

"What are you going to do with the sled?" inquired Nelly, observing that her brother was overhauling the lashings and drag-rope.

"Well, I set a lot o' snares, an' there's no sayin' how many rabbits may have got into 'em. Besides, if the rabbits in them parts are tender-hearted, a lot o' their relations may have died o' grief, so I shall take the sled to fetch 'em all home!"

After breakfast Roy loaded his gun with ball, and putting on his snowshoes, sallied forth with an admonition to his sister to "have a roarin' fire ready to cook a rare feast!"

Nelly laughingly replied, that she would, and so they parted.

The first part of Roy's journey that day led him through a thickly-wooded part of the country. He went along with the quick, yet cautious and noiseless, step of a hunter accustomed to the woods from infancy. His thoughts were busy within him, and far away from the scene in which he moved; yet, such is the force of habit, he never for a moment ceased to cast quick, inquiring glances on each side as he went along. Nothing escaped his observation.

"Oh, if I could only get a deer this day," thought he, "how scrumptious it would be!"

What he meant by "scrumptious" is best known to himself, but at that moment a large deer suddenly — perhaps scrumptiously! — appeared on the brow of a ridge not fifty yards in advance of him. They had been both walking towards each other all that forenoon. Roy, having no powers of scent beyond human powers, did not know the fact, and as the wind was blowing from the deer to the hunter, the former – gifted though he was with scenting powers – was also ignorant of the approaching meeting.

One instant the startled deer stood in bewildered surprise. One instant Roy paused in mute amazement. The next instant the deer wheeled round, while Roy's gun leaped to his shoulder. There was a loud report, followed by reverberating echoes among the hills, and the deer lay dead on the snow.

The young hunter could not repress a shout of joy, for he not only had secured a noble stag, but he had now a sufficiency of food to enable him to resume his homeward journey.

His first impulse was to run back to the hut with the deer's tongue and a few choice bits, to tell Nelly of his good fortune; but, on second thoughts, he resolved to complete the business on which he had started. Leaving the deer where it fell he went on, and found that the snares had been very successful. Some, indeed, had been broken by the strength of the boughs to which they had been fastened, and others remained as he had set them; but above two-thirds of them had each a rabbit hung up by the neck, so that the sled was pretty well loaded when all the snares had been visited.

He had by this time approached the spot where the bear-trap was set, and naturally began to grow a little anxious, for, although his chance of success was very slight, his good fortune that morning had made him more sanguine than usual.

There is a proverb which asserts that "it never rains but it pours." It would seem to be a common experience of mankind that pieces of good fortune, as well as misfortunes, come not singly. Whether the proverb be true or no, this experience was realised by Roy on that day, for he actually did find a bear in his trap! Moreover it was alive, and, apparently, had only just been caught, for it struggled to free itself with a degree of ferocity that was terrible to witness.

It was an ordinary black bear of considerable size and immense strength. Heavy and thick though the trees were that lay on its back and crushed it to the earth, it caused them to shake, leap, and quiver as though they had been endowed with life. Roy was greatly alarmed, for he perceived that at each successive struggle the brute was ridding itself of the superincumbent load, while fierce growls and short gasps indicated at once the wrath and the agony by which it was convulsed.

Roy had neglected to reload his piece after shooting the deer — a most un-hunterlike error, which was the result of excitement. Thinking that he had not time to load, he acted now on the first suggestion of his bold spirit. Resting his gun against a tree, he drew the small axe that hung at his belt and attacked the bear.

The first blow was well delivered, and sank deep into bruin's skull; but that skull was thick, and the brain was not reached. A roar and a furious struggle caused Roy to deliver his second blow with less effect, but this partial failure caused his pugnacity to rise, and he immediately rained down blows on the head and neck of the bear so fast and furious that the snow was speedily covered with blood. In proportion as Roy strove to end the conflict by vigorous and quick blows, the bear tried to get free by furious efforts. He shook the tree-stem that held him down so violently that one of the other trees that rested on it fell off, and thus the load was lightened. Roy observed this, and made a desperate effort to split the bear's skull. In his haste he misdirected the blow, which fell not on the head but on the neck, in which the iron head of the axe was instantly buried — a main artery was severed, and a fountain of blood sprang forth. This was fortunate, for the bear's strength was quickly exhausted, and, in less than two minutes after, it sank dead upon the snow.

Roy sat down to rest and wipe the blood from his hands and garments, and then, cutting off the claws of the animal as a trophy, he left it there for a time. Having now far more than it was possible for him to drag to the hut, he resolved to proceed thither with the rabbits, and bring Nelly back to help him to drag home the deer.

"Well done, Roy," cried Nelly, clapping her hands, when her brother approached with the sled-load of rabbits, "but you are covered with blood. Have you cut yourself?"

She became nervously anxious, for she well knew that a bad cut on a journey costs many a man his life, as it not only disables from continuing the journey but from hunting for provisions.

"All right, Nell, but I've killed a deer — and — and — something else! Come, lass, get on your snowshoes and follow me. We'll drag home the deer, and then see what is to be done with the —"

"Oh, *what* is it? do tell!" cried Nell, eagerly.

"Well, then, it's a bear!"

"Nonsense! — tell me true, now."

"That's the truth, Nell, as you shall see, and here are the claws. Look sharp, now, and let's off."

Away went these two through the snow until they came to where the deer had been left. It was hard work to get it lashed on the sled, and much harder work to drag it over the snow, but by dint of perseverance and resolution they got it home. They were so fatigued, however, that it was impossible to think of doing the same with the bear. This was a perplexing state of things, for Roy had observed a wolf-track when out, and feared that nothing but the bones would be left in the morning.

"What *is* to be done?" said Nelly, with that pretty air of utter helplessness which she was wont to assume when she felt that her brother was the proper person to decide.

Roy pondered a few moments, and then said abruptly, "Camp-out, Nelly."

"Camp-out?"

"Ay, beside the bear — keep it company all night with a big fire to scare away the wolves. We'll put everything into the hut, block up the door, and kindle a huge fire outside that will burn nearly all night. So now, let's go about it at once."

Although Nelly did not much relish the idea of leaving their comfortable hut, and going out to encamp in the snow beside the carcase of a dead bear, she was so accustomed to regard her brother's plans as perfect, and to obey him promptly, that she at once began to assist in the necessary preparations. Having secured everything safely in the hut, and kindled a fire near it, which was large enough to have roasted an ox, they set off for the bear-trap, and reached it in time to scare away a large wolf which was just going to begin his supper on bruin.

An encampment was then made in the usual way, close to the bear-trap, a fire as large as could be conveniently made was kindled, and the brother and sister wrapped themselves in their blankets and lay comfortably down beside it to spend the night there.

CHAPTER XIII.

"Shooskin'."

Next day Roy and Nelly rose with the sun, and spent the forenoon in skinning and cutting up the bear, for they intended to dry part of the meat, and use it on their journey. The afternoon was spent in dragging the various parts to the hut. In the evening Roy proposed that they should go and have a shoosk. Nelly agreed, so they sallied forth to a neighbouring slope with their sledge.

Shoosking, good reader, is a game which is played not only by children but by men and women; it is also played in various parts of the world, such as Canada and Russia, and goes by various names; but we shall adopt the name used by *our* hero and heroine, namely "shoosking." It is very simple, but uncommonly violent, and consists in hauling a sledge to the top of a snow-hill or slope, getting upon it, and sliding down to the bottom. Of course, the extent of violence depends on the steepness of the slope, the interruptions that occur in it, and the nature of the ground at the bottom. We once shoosked with an Indian down a wood-cutter's track, on the side of a steep hill, which had a sharp turn in it, with a pile of firewood at the turn, and a hole in the snow at the bottom, in which were a number of old empty casks. Our great difficulties in this place were to take the turn without grazing the firewood, and to stop our sledges before reaching the hole. We each had separate sledges. For some time we got on famously, but at last *we* ran into the pile of firewood, and tore all the buttons off our coat, and the Indian went down into the hole with a hideous crash among the empty casks; yet, strange to say, neither of us came by any serious damage!

"There's a splendid slope," said Roy, as they walked briskly along the shores of Silver Lake, dragging the sledge after them, "just beyond the big cliff, but I'm afraid it's too much for *you*."

"Oh, *I* can go if you can," said Nell, promptly.

"You've a good opinion of yourself. I guess I could make you sing small if I were to try."

"Then don't try," said Nelly, with a laugh.

"See," continued Roy, "there's the slope; you see it is very steep; we'd go down it like a streak of greased lightnin'; but I don't like to try it."

"Why not? It seems easy enough to me. I'm sure we have gone down as steep places before at home."

"Ay, lass, but not with a round-backed drift like that at the bottom. It has got such a curve that I think it would make us fly right up into the air."

Nelly admitted that it looked dangerous, but suggested that they might make a trial.

"Well, so we will, but I'll go down by myself first," said Roy, arranging the sledge at the summit of a slope, which was full fifty feet high.

"Now, then, pick up the bits tenderly, Nell, if I'm knocked to pieces; here goes, hurrah!"

Roy had seated himself on the sledge, with his feet resting on the head of it, and holding on to the sidelines with both hands firmly. He pushed off as he cheered, and the next moment was flying down the hill at railway speed, with a cloud of snow-drift rolling like steam behind him. He reached the foot, and the impetus sent him up and over the snow-drift or wave, and far out upon the surface of the lake. It is true he made one or two violent swerves in this wild descent, owing to inequalities in the hill, but by a touch of his hands in the snow on either side, he guided the sledge, as with a rudder, and reached the foot in safety.

"May I venture, Roy?" inquired Nell, eagerly, as the lad came panting up the hill.

"Venture! Of course. I rose off the top o' the drift only a little bit, hardly felt the crack at all; come, get you on in front, and I'll sit at yer back an' steer."

Nelly needed no second bidding. She sat down and seized the sidelines of the sledge with a look of what we may call wild expectation; Roy sat down behind her.

"Now, lass, steady, and away we go!"

At the last word they shot from the hilltop like an arrow from a bow. The cloud of snow behind them rolled thicker, for the sledge was more heavily laden than before. Owing to the same cause it plunged into the hollow at the foot of the hill with greater violence, and shot up the slope of the snow-drift and over its crest with such force that it sprung horizontally forward for a few feet in the air, and came to the ground with a crash that extracted a loud gasp from Roy, and a sharp squeak from Nelly. It was found to be so delightful, however, that they tried it again and again, each time becoming more expert, and therefore more confident.

Excessive confidence, however, frequently engenders carelessness. Roy soon became reckless; Nelly waxed fearless. The result was that the former steered somewhat wildly, and finally upset.

Their last "shoosk" that evening was undertaken just as the sun's latest rays were shooting between the hills on the opposite side of Silver Lake, and casting a crimson glow on the hut and the surrounding scenery. Roy had fixed a snowshoe on the outer ridge of the snow-drift, to mark the distance of their last leap from its crest, and had given the sledge an extra push on the way down to increase its impetus. This extra push disconcerted him in steering; he reached the hollow in a sidelong fashion, shot up the slope of the drift waveringly, and left its crest with a swing that not only turned the sledge right round, but also upside down. Of course they were both thrown off, and all three fell into the snow in a condition of dire confusion. Fortunately, no damage was done beyond the shock and the fright, but this accident was sufficient to calm their spirits, and incline them to go home to supper.

"Well, it's great fun, no doubt, but we must turn our minds to more earnest work, for our journey lies before us," said Roy, with the gravity of an Iroquois warrior, as he sat beside the fire that night discussing a bear-steak with his sister. "We have more than enough of fish and meat, you see; a day or two will do to turn our deer and bear into dried meat; the snowshoes are mended, the sledge is in good order, as tonight's work has proved, and all that we've got to do is to start fresh with true bearin's and — hey! for home!"

"I wish I was there," said Nelly, laying down a marrow-bone with a sigh.

"Wishin' ain't enough, Nell."

"I know that, an' I'm ready to work," said Nelly, resuming the bone with a resolute air. "When shall we set out?"

"When we are ready, lass. We shall begin to dry the meat tomorrow, an' as soon as it's fixed — off we'll start. I only hope the cold weather will last, for if it came warm it would go hard with your little feet, Nell. But let's turn in now. Hard work requires a good sleep, an' it may be that we've harder work than we think before us."

CHAPTER XIV.

The Journey Home Resumed and Interrupted.

Three days more and our young friends bade farewell to Silver Lake.

Short though their stay had been, it had proved very pleasant, for it was full of energetic labour and active preparation, besides a great deal of amusement, so that quite a home feeling had been aroused in their minds, and their regret at leaving was considerable.

But after the first few miles of their journey had been accomplished, the feeling of sadness with which they set out wore away, and hopeful anticipations of being home again in a few weeks rendered them cheerful, and enabled them to proceed with vigour. The weather at starting was fine, too, so that the night encampments in the snow were comparatively agreeable, and the progress made during the first few days was satisfactory.

After this, however, the good fortune of our adventurers seemed to desert them. First of all one of Nelly's snowshoes broke down. This necessitated a halt of half a day, in order to have it repaired. Then one of Roy's snowshoes gave way, which caused another halt. After this a heavy snow-storm set in, rendering the walking very difficult, as they sank, snowshoes and all, nearly to the knees at each step. A storm of wind which arose about the same time, effectually stopped their farther advance, and obliged them to take to the shelter of a dense part of the woods and encamp.

During three days and three nights the hurricane raged, and the snow was blown up in the air and whirled about like the foam of the roaring sea; but our wanderers did not feel its effects much, for they had chosen a very sheltered spot at the foot of a large pine, which grew in a hollow, where a cliff on one side and a bluff of wood on the other rendered the blast powerless. Its fierce howling could be heard, however, if not felt; and as the brother and sister lay at the bottom of their hole in the snow, with their toes to the comfortable fire, they chatted much more cheerily than might have been expected in the midst of such a scene, and gazed upward from time to time with comparative indifference at the dark clouds and snow-drifts that were rushing madly overhead.

On the fourth day the gale subsided almost as quickly as it had arisen, and Roy announced that it was his intention to start. In a few minutes everything was packed up and ready.

"I say, Nell," said Roy, just as they were about to leave the camp, "don't the sled look smaller than it used to?"

"So it does, Roy; but I suppose it's because we have eaten so much during the last three days."

Roy shook his head, and looked carefully round the hole they were about to quit.

"Don't know, lass; it seems to me as if somethin' was a-wantin'. Did ye pack your own bundle very tight?"

"Yes; I think I did it tighter than usual, but I'm not very sure."

"Hum — that's it, no doubt — we've packed the sled tighter, and eaten it down. Well, let's off now."

So saying, Roy threw the lines of the sledge over his shoulder and led the way, followed by his sister, whose only burden was a light blanket, fastened as a bundle to her shoulders, and a small tin can, which hung at her belt.

The country through which they passed that day was almost destitute of wood, being a series of undulating plains, with clumps of willows and stunted trees scattered over it like islets in the sea. The land lay in a succession of ridges, or steppes, which descended from the elevated region they were leaving, and many parts of these ridges terminated abruptly in sheer precipices from forty to sixty feet high.

The sun shone with dazzling brilliancy, insomuch that the travellers' eyes became slightly affected by snow-blindness. This temporary blindness is very common in these regions, and ranges from the point of slight dazzlement to that of total blindness; fortunately it is curable by the removal of the cause — the bright light of the sun on pure snow. Esquimaux use "goggles" or spectacles made of wood, with a narrow slit in them as a preventive of snow-blindness.

At first neither Roy nor Nelly felt much inconvenience, but

towards evening they could not see as distinctly as usual. One consequence of this was, that they approached a precipice without seeing it. The snow on its crest was so like to the plain of snow extending far below, that it might have deceived one whose eyesight was not in any degree impaired.

The first intimation they had of their danger was the giving way of the snow that projected over the edge of the precipice. Roy fell over headlong, dragging the sledge with him. Nelly, who was a few feet behind him, stood on the extreme edge of the precipice, with the points of her snowshoes projecting over it. Roy uttered a cry as he fell, and his sister stopped short. A shock of terror blanched her cheek and caused her heart to stand still. She could not move or cry for a few seconds, then she uttered a loud shriek and shrank backwards.

There chanced to be a stout bush or tree growing on the face of the cliff, not ten feet below the spot where the snow-wreath had broken off. Roy caught at this convulsively, and held on. Fortunately the line on his shoulder broke, and the sledge fell into the abyss below. Had this not happened, it is probable that he would have been dragged from his hold of the bush. As it was, he maintained his hold, and hung for a few seconds suspended in the air. Nelly's shriek revived him from the gush of deadly terror that seized him when he fell. He grasped the boughs above him, and was quickly in a position of comparative security among the branches of the bush.

"All right, Nell," he gasped, on hearing her repeat her cry of despair. "I'm holdin' on quite safe. Keep back from the edge, lass — there's no fear o' me."

"Are you sure, Roy?" cried Nelly, trembling very much, as she stretched forward to try to catch sight of her brother.

"Ay, quite sure; but I can't get up, for there's six feet o' smooth rock above me, an' nothin' to climb up by."

"Oh! what *shall* I do!" cried Nelly.

"Don't get flurried — that's the main thing, lass. Let me think — ay, that's it — you've got your belt?"

"Yes."

"Well, take it off and drop the end over to me; but lie down on your breast, and be careful."

Nelly obeyed, and in a few seconds the end of the worsted belt that usually encircled her waist was dangling almost within reach of her brother. This belt was above five feet long. Roy wore one of similar material and length. He untied it, and then sought to lay hold of the other. With some difficulty and much risk of falling he succeeded, and fastened his own belt to it firmly.

"Now, Nell, haul up a little bit — hold! enough."

"What am I to do now?" asked Nell, piteously; "I cannot pull you up, you know."

"Of course not; but take your snowshoe and dig down to the rocks — you'll find somethin', I dare say, to tie the belts to. Cheer up, lass, and go at it."

Thus encouraged, the active little girl soon cleared away the snow until she reached the ground, where she found several roots of shrubs that seemed quite strong enough for her purpose. To one of these she tied the end of her belt, and Roy, being an athletic lad, hauled himself up, hand over hand, until he gained a place of safety.

"But the sledge is gone," cried Nelly, pausing suddenly in the midst of her congratulations.

"Ay, and the grub," said Roy, with a blank look.

This was indeed too true, and on examination it was found that things were even worse than had been anticipated, for the sledge had fallen on a ledge, half way down the precipice, that was absolutely inaccessible either from above or below. An hour was spent in ascertaining this, beyond all doubt, and then Roy determined to return at once to their last encampment to gather the scraps they had thrown away or left behind as useless.

That night they went supperless to rest. Next morning, they set out with heavy hearts for the encampment of the previous day. On reaching it, and searching carefully, they found that one of the bundles of dry meat had been forgotten. This accounted for the lightness of the sledge, and, at the same time, revived their drooping spirits.

"What is to be done now?" inquired Nelly.

"Return to Silver Lake," said Roy, promptly. "We must go back, fish and hunt again until we have another supply o' grub, and then begin our journey once more."

Sadly and slowly they retraced their steps. Do what he would Roy could not cheer up his sister's spirits. She felt that her back was turned towards her father's house — her mother's home — and every step took her farther from it.

It was a lovely evening, about sunset, when they reached Silver Lake, and found the hut as they had left it, and enough of old scraps of provisions to afford a sufficient meal.

That night they ate their supper in a more cheerful frame of mind. Next day they breakfasted almost with a feeling of heartiness, and when they went out to resume their fishing, and to set snares and make traps, the old feeling of hopefulness returned. Ere long, hope became again so strong in their ardent young hearts, that they laughed and talked and sported as they had done during the period of their first residence there.

At first they were so anxious to make up the lost quantity of food that they did little else but fish, hunt, and dry their provisions when obtained; but after a few days they had procured such an ample supply that they took to shoosking again — having succeeded in making a new sledge. But a thaw came suddenly and spoiled all their fish. A wolf carried off the greater part of their dried meat one day while they were absent from the hut. After this the frost set in with extreme violence, game became more scarce, and fish did not take the bait so readily, so that, although they procured more than enough for present consumption, they were slow in accumulating a travelling store; and thus it came to pass that November found Roy and Nelly still toiling wearily, yet hopefully, on the shores of Silver Lake.

CHAPTER XV.

The Massacre.

We must return now to Robin Gore and his wife, who, on the morning on which we re-introduce them to the reader, were standing in the trading store of Fort Enterprise, conversing earnestly with Black, the Indian, who has been already mentioned at the beginning of our tale. The wife of the latter — the White Swan — was busily engaged in counting over the pack of furs that lay open on the counter, absorbed, apparently, in an abstruse calculation as to how many yards of cloth and strings of beads they would purchase.

"Well, I'm glad that's fixed, anyhow," said Robin to his wife, as he turned to the Indian with a satisfied air, and addressed him in his native tongue, "it's a bargain, then, that you an' Slugs go with me on this expedition, is't so?"

"The Black Swan is ready," replied the Indian, quietly, "and he thinks that Slugs will go too — but the white hunter is self-willed; he has a mouth — ask himself."

"Ay, ye don't like to answer for him," said Robin, with a smile; "assuredly Slugs has his own notions, and holds to 'em; but I'll ask him. He is to be here this night, with a deer, I hope, for there are many mouths to fill."

Black Swan, who was a tall, taciturn, and powerful Indian, here glanced at his wife, who was, like most Indian women, a humble-looking and not very pretty or clean creature. Turning again to Robin, he said, in a low, soft voice —

"The White Swan is not strong, and she is not used to be alone."

"I understand you," said Robin; "she shall come to the Fort, and be looked after. You won't object to take her in, Molly, when we're away?"

"Object, Robin," said Molly, with a smile, which was accompanied by a sigh, "I'll only be too glad to have her company."

"Well, then, that's settled; and now, Black Swan, I may as well tell you what coorse I mean to follow out in this sarch for my child'n. You know already that four white men — strangers — have come to the Fort, an' are now smokin' their pipes in the hall, but you don't know that one on 'em is my own brother Jefferson; Jeff, I've bin used to call him. Jeff's bin a harem-scarem feller all his life — active and able enough, an' good natur'd too, but he never could stick to nothin', an' so he's bin wanderin' about the world till grey hairs have begun to show on him, without gettin' a home or a wife. The last thing he tried was stokin' a steamboat on the Mississippi; but the boat blew up, pitched a lot o' the passengers into the water, an' the rest o' them into the next world. Jeff was always in luck with his life; he's lost everythin' over an' over again but that. He was one o' the lot as was blowed into the water, so, when he come up he swamed ashore, an' come straight away here to visit me, bringin' three o' the blowed-up passengers with him. The three are somethin' like himself; good for nothin'; an' I'd rather have their room than their company at most times. Hows'ever, just at this time I'm very glad they've come, for I'll leave them in charge o' the Fort, and set off to look for the child'n in two days from this. I'll take Walter and Larry wi' me, for brother Jeff is able enough to manage the trade if redskins come; he can fight too, if need be. The Gore family could always do that, so ye needn't be afraid, Molly."

"I'll not be afraid, Robin, but I'll be anxious about ye."

"That's nat'ral, lass, but it can't be helped. Well, then," continued Robin, "the five of us will start for the Black Hills. I've bin told by a red-skin who comed here last week that he an' his tribe had had a scrim-mage with Hawk an' the reptiles that follow him. He says that there was a white boy an' a white girl with Hawk's party, an' from his account of 'em I'm sartin sure it's my Roy and Nelly. God help 'em! 'but,' says he, 'they made their escape durin' the attack, an' we followed our enemies so far that we didn't think it worth while to return to look for 'em, so I'm convinced they made for the Black Hills, nigh which Hawk was attacked, an' if we follow 'em up there we may find 'em alive yet, mayhap.'"

Poor Robin's voice became deeper and less animated as he spoke, and the last word was uttered with hesitation and in a whisper.

"O Robin, Robin!" exclaimed Mrs. Gore, throwing her arms suddenly round her husband's neck, and hiding her sobbing face in his breast, "d'ye think they can *still* be alive?"

"Come, Molly," said Robin, commanding his feelings with a great effort, "han't ye often read to me that wi' God all things is possible?"

The poor woman thanked God in her heart, for up to that day Robin had never once quoted Scripture in his efforts to comfort her.

"Was Wapaw with Hawk when they were attacked?" inquired the Black Swan.

"Wapaw is dead," said a deep voice, as the huge form of a western hunter darkened the little doorway, and the next moment Slugs strode into the store, and quietly seated himself on the counter.

"Dead!" exclaimed Robin, as he shook the hunter's proffered hand.

"Ay, dead! Have ye no word of welcome for a chum after a month's absence?" said Slugs, holding out his horny hand to the Black Swan, who gravely grasped and shook it.

"You redskins are a queer lot," said Slugs, with a grin, "yer as stiff as a rifle ramrod to look at, but there's warm and good stuff in 'ee for all that."

"But what about Wapaw?" inquired Mrs. Gore, anxiously; "surely he's not dead."

"If he's not dead he's not livin', for I saw Hawk himself, not four weeks ago, shoot him and follow him up with his tomahawk, and then heard their shout as they killed him. Where did he say he was goin' when he left you?"

"He said he would go down to the settlements to see the missionaries, an' that he thought o' lookin' in on the fur-traders that set up a fort last year, fifty miles to the south'ard o' this."

"Ay, just so," said Slugs; "I was puzzled to know what he was doin' thereaway, and that explains it. He's dead now, an' so are the fur-traders he went to see. I'll tell ye all about it if you'll give me baccy enough to fill my pipe. I ran out o't three days agone, an' ha' bin smokin' tealeaves an' bark, an' all sorts o' trash. Thank 'ee; that's a scent more sweet nor roses."

As he said this the stout hunter cut up the piece of tobacco which

Robin at once handed to him, and rolled it with great zest between his palms. When the pipe was filled and properly lighted, he leaned his back against an unopened bale of goods that lay on the counter, and drawing several whiffs, began his narrative.

"You must know that I made tracks for the noo fur-tradin' post when I left you, Black Swan, about a month ago. I hadn't much of a object; it was mainly cooriosity as took me there. I got there all right, an' was sittin' in the hall chattin' wi' the head man — Macdonell they called him — about the trade and the Injuns. Macdonell's two little child'n was playin' about, a boy an' a girl, as lively as kittens, an' his wife — a good-lookin' young 'ooman — was lookin' arter 'em, when the door opens, and in stalks a long-legged Injun. It was Wapaw. Down he sat in front o' the fireplace, an' after some palaver an' a pipe — for your Injuns'll never tell all they've got to say at once — he tells Macdonell that there was a dark plot hatchin' agin' him — that Hawk, a big rascal of his own tribe, had worked upon a lot o' reptiles like hisself, an' they had made up their minds to come an' massacre everybody at the Fort, and carry off the goods.

"At first Macdonell didn't seem to believe the Injun, but when I told him I knowed him, an' that he was a trustworthy man, he was much troubled, an' in doubt what to do. Now, it's quite clear to me that Hawk must have somehow found out or suspected that Wapaw was goin' to 'peach on him, an' that he had followed his trail close up; for in less than an hour arter Wapaw arrived, an' while we was yet sittin' smokin' by the fire, there was a most tremendous yell outside. I know'd it for the war-whoop o' the redskins, so I jumped up an' cocked my rifle. The others jumped up too, like lightnin'; an' Mrs. Macdonell she got hold o' her girlie in her arms an' was runnin' across the hall to her own room, when the door was knocked off its hinges, and fell flat on the floor. Before it had well-nigh fallen I got sight o' somethin', an' let drive. The yell that follered told me I had spoilt somebody's aim. A volley was poured on us next moment, an' a redskin jumped in, but Wapaw's tomahawk sent him out again with a split skull. Before they could reload — for the stupid fools had all fired together — I had the door up, and a heavy table shoved agin it. Then I turned round, to load agin; while I was doin' this, I observed poor Macdonell on his knees beside his wife, so I went to them an' found that the wife an' girl were stone dead — both shot through the heart with the same ball.

"As soon as Macdonell saw this he rose up quietly, but with a look on his face sich as I never see in a man 'xcept when he means to stick at nothin'. He got hold of his double-barrelled gun, an' stuck a scalpin' knife an' an axe in his belt.

"'Git on my back, Tommy,' says he to his little boy, who was cryin' in a corner.

"Tommy got up at once, an' jumped on his dad's back. All this time the redskins were yellin' round the house like fiends, an' batterin' the door, so that it was clear it couldn't stand long.

"'Friends,' said he turnin' to me an' Wapaw, an' a poor terrified chap that was the only one o' his men as chanced to be in the house at the time, 'friends, it's every man for himself now; I'll cut my way though them, or — '. He stopped short, an' took hold o' his axe in one hand, an' his gun in the other. 'Are ye ready?' says he. We threw forward our rifles an' cocked 'em; Macdonell — he was a big, strong man — suddenly upset the table; the savages dashed in the door with sich force that three or four o' 'em fell sprawlin' on the floor. We jumped over these before they could rise, and fired a volley, which sent three or four o' the reptiles behind on their backs. We got into the bush without a scratch, an' used our legs well, I can tell 'ee. They fired a volley after us, which missed us all except poor Tommy. A bullet entered his brain, an' killed him dead. For some time his father would not drop him, though I told him he was quite dead; but his weight kept him from runnin' fast, an' we heard the redskins gainin' on us, so at last Macdonell put the boy down tenderly under a bush. Me and Wapaw stopped to fire an' keep the reptiles back, but they fired on us, and Wapaw fell. I tried to lift him, but he struggled out o' my arms. Poor fellow! he was a brave man; and I've no doubt did it a-purpose, knowin' that I couldn't run fast enough with him. Just then I saw Hawk come jumpin' and yellin' at us, followed by two or three dozen redskins, all flourishin' their tomahawks. Macdonell and me turned to die fightin' alongside o' our red comrade, but Wapaw suddenly sprang up, uttered a shout of defiance, an' dashed into the bush. The Injuns were after him in a moment, and before we could get near them a yell of triumph told us that it was too late, so we turned and bolted in different directions.

"I soon left them behind me, but I hung about the place for a day or two to see if Macdonell should turn up, or any of his men. I even went back to the Fort after the reptiles had left it. They had burned it down, an' I saw parts o' the limbs o' the poor wife and child lyin' among the half-burned goods that they weren't able to carry away with them."

CHAPTER XVI.

Vengeance.

The terrible tale which was related by Slugs had the effect of changing Robin Gore's plans. He resolved to pursue the murderers, and inflict summary punishment on them before setting off on the contemplated search for his lost children, and he was all the more induced to do this that there was some hope he might be able to obtain a clue to their whereabouts from some of the prisoners whom he hoped to seize.

It might be thought by some a rash step for him to take — the pursuit of a band of about fifty savages with a party of six men. But backwood hunters were bold fellows in those days, and Indians were by no means noted for reckless courage. Six stout, resolute, and well-armed men were, in Robin's opinion, quite a match for fifty redskins!

He could not muster more than six, because it was absolutely necessary to leave at least three men to guard Fort Enterprise. Robin therefore resolved to leave his brother Jeff to look after it, with two of the strangers; and Jeff accepted the charge with pleasure, saying he "would defend the place agin a hundred red reptiles." The third stranger — a man named Stiff — he resolved to take with him.

The war-party, when mustered, consisted of Robin Gore, his nephew Walter, Larry O'Dowd, the Black Swan, Slugs the hunter, and Stiff the stranger. Armed to the teeth, these six put on their snowshoes the following morning, and set forth on their journey in silence.

Now this change of plans was — all unknown to Robin — the means of leading him towards, instead of away from, his lost little ones. For Roy and Nelly had travelled so far during their long wanderings from the Black Hills — the place where they escaped from the Indians — that they were at that time many long miles away from them in another direction. In fact, if Robin had carried out his original plan of search, he would have been increasing the distance between himself and his children every step he took!

Not knowing this, however, and being under the impression that each day's march lessened his chance of ultimately finding his lost ones, he walked along, mile after mile, and day after day, in stern silence.

On the third day out, towards evening, the party descried a thin line of blue smoke rising above the treetops. They had reached an elevated and somewhat hilly region, so that the ground favoured their approach by stealth, nevertheless, fearing to lose their prey, they resolved to wait till dark, and take their enemies, if such they should turn out to be, by surprise.

Soon after sunset Robin gave the word to advance. Each man of the party laid aside his blanket, and left his provisions, &c., in the encampment, taking with him his arms only.

"I need not say that there must be no speaking, and that we must tread lightly. You're up to redskin ways as well as me, except mayhap our friend Stiff here."

Stiff who was a tall Yankee, protested that he could "chaw up his tongue, and go as slick as a feline mouser."

On nearing the fire, they made a *détour* to examine the tracks that led to it, and found from their number and other signs that it was indeed Hawk's party.

Robin advanced alone to reconnoitre. On returning, he said —

"It's just the reptiles; there's forty of 'em if there's one, an' they've got a white man bound with 'em; no doubt from what you said of him, Slugs, it's Macdonell; but I don't see Wapaw. I fear me that his days are over. Now, then, lads, here's our plan: we'll attack them from six different points at once. We'll all give the war-whoop at the same moment, takin' the word from Walter there, who's got a loud pipe of his own, then when the varmints start to their feet — for I don't like the notion o' firin' at men off their guard — Walter, Larry, an' Stiff will fire. Black Swan, Slugs, an' I will reserve our fire while you reload; the reptiles will scatter, of course, an' we'll give 'em a volley an' a united yell as they cut stick, that'll keep 'em from waitin' for more."

The plan thus hastily sketched was at once carried out. Advancing stealthily to their several stations, the six men, as it were, surrounded the savages, who, not dreaming of pursuit, had neglected to place sentinels round the camp. When Walter's loud "halloo!" rang in their ears, the whole band sprang to their feet, and seized their arms, but three shots laid three of them dead on the ground. As they fled right and left the reserve fired, and shot three others, among whom was Hawk himself. Black Swan had picked him out, and shot him through the head. Before they were quite out of shot, the three who had first fired had reloaded and fired again with some effect, for blood was afterwards observed on the snow.

Slugs now made a rush into the camp to unbind Macdonell, but to his horror he discovered that a knife was plunged up to the handle in his breast, and that he was almost dead. Hawk had evidently committed this cowardly deed on the first alarm, for the knife was known to be his. Macdonell tried hard to speak, but all that he was able to say was, "Wapaw, wounded, escaped — follow." Then his head fell back, and he died. From the few words thus uttered, however, the pursuers concluded that Wapaw was not dead, but wounded, and that he had escaped.

"If that be so," said Walter, "then they must have been on Wapaw's tracks, an' if we search we shall find 'em, an' may follow 'em up."

"True," said Slugs, "and the sooner we're away from this the better, for the reptiles may return, and find us not so strong a band as they think."

Acting on this advice, the whole party set off at once. Wapaw's track was soon discovered, being, of course, a solitary one, and in advance of his enemies, who were in pursuit. Following the track with untiring vigour, the party found that it led them out of the lower country into a region high up amongst the hills.

CHAPTER XVII.

The Pursuit.

"Wapaw must have worked hard, for we should have overhauled him by this time," said Walter to his uncle on the evening of the next day, as they plodded steadily along through the snow.

"I would give up the pursuit," said Robin, somewhat gloomily, "for it's losin' time that might be better spent on another search; but it won't do to leave the crittur, for if he's badly wounded he may die for want o' help."

"Guess he can't be very bad, else he'd niver travel so fast," observed Stiff, who, now that the chief murderer was punished, did not care much to go in search of the wounded Indian.

"When a man thinks a band o' yellin' redskins are follerin' up his trail," said Slugs, "he's pretty sure to travel fast, wounded or not wounded — leastways if he's able. But I don't think we'll have to go much farther now, for I've noticed that his stride ain't so long as it was, and that's a sartin sure sign that he's failin'; I only hope he won't go under before we find him."

"Niver a fear o' that," said Larry O'Dowd, with a grin. "I've seed him as far gone as any one iver I comed across, wi' starvation; but the way that fellow walked into the grub when he got the chance was wonderful to behold! I thought he'd ait me out o' the house entirely; and he put so much flesh on his bones in a week or two that he was able to go about his business, though he warn't no fatter when he began to ait than a consumptive darnin' needle. True for ye — it's naither walkin', starvin', nor cowld, as'll kill Wapaw."

"What does the Black Swan think?" inquired Robin.

"We shall see Wapaw when the sun is low tomorrow," replied the Indian.

"Mayhap we shall," quoth Robin, "but it behooves us to get the steam up for tomorrow: so, comrades, as there's a good clump o' timber here away, we'll camp."

Robin threw down his bundle as he spoke, and his example was at once followed by the others, each of whom set to work vigorously to assist in preparing the encampment.

They had all the requisite implements for this purpose, having returned, after the attack on the Indians, for the things they had left behind them.

"It's a pity that we shall have to keep watch tonight," said Walter; "one of us will have to do it, I fancy; for though I don't believe these murderin' redskins have pluck to attack us, it would not do to trust to that."

Slugs, to whom this remark was addressed, lowered the axe with which he was about to fell a neighbouring tree for firewood.

"That's true," said he, looking round him in all directions; "hold on, comrades, yonder's a mound with a bare top, we'd better camp there. Makin' a big blaze on sitch a place'll show the red reptiles we don't care a gun-flint for them, and they'll not dare to come near, so we won't have to watch."

"Arrah! an' a purty spot it'll be for the blackyirds to shoot us all aisy as we're sottin' at supper," exclaimed Larry O'Dowd.

"Doubtless there's a hollow on it," rejoined Slugs, "for the top is flat."

"Humph! maybe," growled Larry, who still seemed to object; but, as the rest of the party were willing to adopt the suggestion, he said no more, and they all went to the top of the little mound, which commanded a clear view of the surrounding country.

As Slugs had surmised, there was a slight hollow on the summit of the mound, which effectually screened the party from any one who might wish to fire at them from below; and as there was no other mound in the immediate neighbourhood, they felt quite secure. Huge logs were cut and carried to the top of the mound, the snow was cleared out of the hole, pine branches were spread over it, the fire was kindled, the kettle put on and filled with snow, and soon Larry O'Dowd was involved in the heat, steam, smoke, and activities of preparing supper, while his comrades spread out their blankets and lay down to smoke with their arms ready beside them.

The fire roared up into the wintry sky, causing the mound to resemble the cone or crater of a volcano, which could be seen for miles round. Ever and anon, while supper was being eaten, the Black Swan or Slugs would rise, and going stealthily to the edge of the mound would peep cautiously over, to make sure that none of their enemies were approaching.

Immediately after supper, they all lay down to sleep, but, for a time, each motionless form that lay rolled tightly in its blanket like an Egyptian mummy, sent a series of little puffs from its head. At last the stars came out, and the pipes dropped from each sleeper's lips. Then the moon rose — a circumstance which rendered their position still more secure — and the fire sank low. But Slugs was too cautious a hunter to trust entirely to the alleged cowardice of the savages. He knew well that many, indeed most of the redskins, bad as well as good, had quite enough of mere brute courage to make them dare and risk a good deal for the sake of scalping a white hunter, so he rose once or twice during the night to replenish the fire and take a look round; and as often as he rose for these purposes, so often did he observe the glittering eye of the Black Swan glaring round the encampment, although its owner never once moved from his recumbent posture.

Thus the night was spent. The first glimmer of daylight found the whole party up and equipped for the journey.

They did not breakfast before setting out, as they preferred to take their morning meal later in the day. Few words were spoken. At that early hour, and in the sleepy condition which usually results from a *very* early start, men are seldom inclined to talk. Only one or two monosyllables were uttered as each man rolled up his blanket with his share of the provisions in it, and fastened on his snowshoes. A few minutes later Robin led the way down the slope, and the whole party marched off in single file, and re-entered the woods.

CHAPTER XVIII.

Interesting though Puzzling Discoveries.

About eight o'clock they halted for breakfast, which Larry O'Dowd prepared with his accustomed celerity, and assisted to consume with his wonted voracity.

"There's nothin' like aitin' when yer hungry," observed Larry, with his mouth full.

"'Xcept drinking when you're dry," said Stiff, ironically.

"Now I don't agree with ye," retorted Larry; "I used to think so wance, before I left the owld country — my blissin' rest on it. I used to think there was nothin' like drink, an' sure I was right, for there niver *was* anythin' like it for turnin' a poor man into a baste; but when I comed into the woods here I couldn't get drink for love or money, an' sure I found, after a while, I didn't need it, and got on better widout it, an' enjoyed me life more for want of it. Musha! it's little I care for drink now; but, och! I've a mortal love for aitin'!"

It needed not Larry's assurance to convince his hearers of the fact, for he consumed nearly twice as much dried meat as any of his comrades.

"Well, if ye don't drink gin-sling or cocktail," said Stiff, "you're mighty hard on the tea."

"True for ye, Stiff, it was the fav'rite tipple o' me owld mother, an' I'm fond of it on that score, not to mention other raisins of a private natur'."

"Couldn't ye make these reasons public?" said Walter.

"Unpossible!" said Larry, with much gravity, as he helped himself to another can of tea.

"Come, time's up," said Robin abruptly, as he rose to put on his snowshoes.

Larry swallowed the tea at a draught, the others rose promptly, and in a few minutes more they were again on the march.

Towards noon they issued out of the woods upon a wide undulating country, which extended, as far as the eye could see, to faint blue mountains in the distance. This region was varied in character and extremely beautiful. The undulations of the land resembled in some places the waves of the sea. In other places there were clumps of trees like islets. Elsewhere there were hollows in which lakelets and ponds evidently existed, but the deep snow covered all these with a uniform carpet. In some parts the ground was irregular and broken by miniature hills, where there were numerous abrupt and high precipices.

The party were approaching one of the latter in the afternoon, when Robin suddenly paused and pointed to a projecting ledge on the face of one of the cliffs.

"What would ye say yonder objic' was?" he inquired of Slugs.

The hunter shaded his eyes with his hand, and remained silent for a few seconds.

"It *looks* like a sled," said he, dropping his hand, "but how it got thar' would puzzle even a redskin to tell, for there's no track up to that ledge."

"It *is* a sled," said Black Swan, curtly.

"An' how came it there?" asked Robin.

"It fell from the top," replied the Indian.

"Right, lad, yer right!" said Slugs, who had taken another long look at the object in question; "I see somethin' like a broken tree near the top o' the precipice. I hope Wapaw hain't gone an' tumbled over that cliff."

This supposition was received in silence and with grave looks, for all felt that the thing was not impossible, but the Indian shook his head.

"Come, Black Swan," said Walter, "you don't agree with us — what think ye?"

"Wapaw had no sled with him," replied the Indian.

"Right again!" cried Slugs; "I do believe my sense is forsakin' me; an Injun baby might have thought of that, for his tracks are plain enough. Hows'ever, let's go see, for it's o' no use standin' here guessin'."

The party at once advanced to the foot of the precipice, and for nearly an hour they did their utmost to ascend to the ledge on which the sledge lay, but their efforts were in vain. The rock was everywhere too steep and smooth to afford foothold.

"It won't do," said Larry, wiping the perspiration from his brow; "av we had wings we might — , but we hain't got 'em, so it's o' no manner o' use tryin'."

"We shall try from the top now," said Robin. "If anybody *has* tumbled over, the poor crittur may be alive yet, for all we know."

They found their efforts to descend from the top of the precipice equally fruitless and much more dangerous, and although they spent a long time in the attempt, and taxed their wits to the utmost, they were ultimately compelled to leave the place and continue their journey without attaining their object.

One discovery was made, however. It was ascertained by the old marks in the snow at the edge of the precipice that, whatever members of the party who owned the sledge had tumbled over, at least two of them had escaped, for their track — faint and scarcely discernible — was traced for some distance. It was found, also, that Wapaw's track joined this old one. The wounded Indian had fallen upon it not far from the precipice, and, supposing, no doubt, that it would lead him to some encampment, he had followed it up. Robin and his men also followed it — increasing their speed as much as possible.

Night began to descend again, but Wapaw was not overtaken, despite the Black Swan's prophecy. This, however, was not so much owing to the miscalculation of the Indian, as to the fact that a great deal of time had been lost in their futile endeavour to reach the sledge that had fallen over the precipice.

About sunset they came to a place where the track turned suddenly at a right angle and entered the bushes.

"Ha! the first travellers must have camped here, and Wapaw has followed their example," said Robin, as he pushed aside the bushes. "Just so, here's the place, but the ashes are cold, so I fear we are not so near our Injun friend as we could wish."

"Well, it can't be helped," cried Stiff, throwing down his bundle; "we've had plenty o' walkin' for one day, so I vote for supper right off."

"I second the motion," said Walter, seizing his axe, "seein' that the camp is ready made to hand. Now, Larry, get your pot ready."

"Sure it's stuffed full a'ready — an' I only wish I was in the same state," said the Irishman, as he pressed the snow tightly into a tin kettle, and hung it over the fire, which Slugs had just kindled.

The supper scene of the previous night was, in most of its details, enacted over again; but it was resolved that each of the party should keep watch for an hour, as, if the Indians had followed, there was a possibility of their having gained on them during the delay at the precipice.

Before the watch was set, however, and while all the party were enjoying their pipes after supper, the Black Swan suddenly exclaimed, "Ho!" and pointed with his finger to something which peeped out of the snow at Larry's elbow, that volatile individual having uncovered it during some of his eccentric movements.

"It's only an owld mocassin," said Larry, plucking the object from the snow as he spoke; "some Injun lad has throw'd it away for useless."

"Hand it here," said Robin, re-lighting his pipe, which had gone out.

Larry tossed the mocassin to his leader, who eyed it carelessly for a moment. Suddenly he started, and, turning the mocassin over, examined it with close and earnest attention. Then he smiled, as if at his passing anxiety, and dropped it on the ground.

"It reminded me," said he to Walter, "of my Nelly, for it has something of the same shape that she was fond of, an' for a moment I was foolish enough to think it might ha' belonged to the dear child, but — . Come, Larry, have 'ee got any more tea there?"

"Is it tay ye want? faix, then, it's little more nor laves that's remainin'," said Larry, draining the last drops into a pannikin; "well, there's about half a mug-full, afther all; it's wonderful what can be got out o' it sometimes by squaazin' the pot."

"Hand it over, that's enough," said Robin, "thank 'ee, lad — here's luck."

He drained the pannikin as though it had been a glass of rum, and, smacking his lips, proceeded leisurely to refill his pipe.

"Are ye sure it's *not* one of Nelly's old mocassins?" asked Walter, as he eyed the little shoe earnestly.

"Sure enough, nephy, I would know her mother's make among ten thousand, an' although that one is oncommon like it in some respec's, it ain't one o' *hers*."

"But Nelly might have made it herself," suggested Walter, "and that would account for its bein' like her mother's in the make."

Robin shook his head. "Not likely," said he. "The child didn't use to make mocassins. I'm not sure if she could do it at all; besides she was last heard of miles and miles away from here in another direction. No, no, Walter lad, we mustn't let foolish fancies bother us. However, the sight o' this has fixed me to push on tomorrow as hard as I can lay my legs to it, for if Wapaw's alive we can't fail to come up wi' him afore sundown; and I'm keen to turn about an' go after my children. I'll push on by myself if ye don't care to keep up wi me."

This latter remark was made to Stiff, whose countenance indicated that he had no desire to undertake a harder day's march than usual. The effect of the remark was to stir up all the Yankee's pride.

"I'll tell 'ee what it is, *Mister* Gore," said he, tartly; "you may think yourself an oncommon hard walker, but Obadiah Stiff is not the man to cave in to any white man alive. I don't care to go trampin' over the country day after day, like the Wandering Jew, after a redskin, as, I'll go bound, ain't no better than the rest o' his kind; but if ye want to see which of our legs is the best pair o' compasses, I'll walk with ye from here to hereafter, I guess, or anywhar else ye choose; if I don't, then my name ain't Stiff."

"It would be well av it worn't Stiff, for ye've no reason to be proud o't," observed Larry O'Dowd, with a grin; "don't spake so loud, man, but shut up yer potatie trap and go to roost. Ye'll need it all if ye wouldn't like to fall behind tomorrow. There now, don't reply; ye've no call to make me yer father confessor, and apologise for boastin'; good night, an' go to slape!"

The rest of the party, who had lain down, laughed at this sally, and Stiff, on consideration, thought it best to laugh too. In a few minutes every one in the encampment was sound asleep, with the exception of Robin Gore, who took the first hour of watching, and who sat beside the sinking fire like a Indian in earnest meditation, with his eyes resting dreamily on the worn-out mocassin.

CHAPTER XIX.

Short Allowance, and a Surprise.

Once again we return to Silver Lake; but here we do not find affairs as we left them. True, Roy and Nelly are still there, the hut is as snug as it used to be, and the scenery as beautiful, but provisions have begun to fail, and an expression of real anxiety clouds the usually cheerful countenance of Roy, while reflected anxiety sits on the sweet little face of Nell. The winter is far advanced, and the prospect of resuming the journey home is farther off than ever.

One morning Roy entered the hut with a slow step and a sad countenance.

"Nell," said he, throwing down a small fish which he had just caught, "things look very bad now; seems to me that we'll starve here. Since we broke the long line I've only caught little things like *that*; there's no rabbits in the snares — I looked at every one this mornin' — and, as for deer, they seem to have said good-bye for the winter. I thought of goin' out with the gun this forenoon, but I think it a'nt o' no use, for I was out all yesterday without seeing a feather or a hoofprint."

The tone in which Roy said this, and the manner in which he flung himself down on the ground beside the fire, alarmed his sister greatly, so that she scarcely knew what to say.

"Don't know what's to be done at all," continued Roy somewhat peevishly.

This was so unlike himself that the little girl felt a strong tendency to burst into tears, but she restrained herself. After a short silence, she said somewhat timidly —

"Don't you think we might try to pray?"

"What's the use," said Roy quickly; "I'm sure I've prayed often and often, and so have you, but nothin's come of it."

It was quite evident that Roy was in a state of rebellion. This was the first time Nelly had suggested *united* prayer to her brother; she did it timidly, and the rebuff caused her to shrink within herself.

Roy's quick eye observed the shrinking; he repented instantly, and, drawing Nelly to him, laid her head on his breast.

"Forgive me, Nell, I shouldn't have said it; for, after all, we've had everything given to us here that we have needed up to this time. Come, I *will* pray with you."

They both got upon their knees at once, but, strive as he might, not a word would cross Roy's lips for several minutes. Nelly raised her head and looked at him.

"God help us!" he ejaculated.

"For Jesus' sake," murmured Nelly.

They both said "Amen" to these words, and these were all their prayers.

Roy's rebellion of heart was gone now, but his feelings were not yet calmed. He leaped up, and, raising his sister, kissed her almost violently.

"Now, lass, we *have* prayed, and I *do* believe that God will answer us; so I'll take my gun and snowshoes, an' off to the woods to look for a deer. See that you have a roarin' fire ready to roast him three hours hence."

Nelly smiled through her tears and said she would, while Roy slipped his feet through the lines of his snowshoes, threw his powder-horn and bullet-pouch over his shoulder, seized his gun, and sallied forth with a light step.

When he was gone, Nelly began actively to prepare for the fulfilment of her promise. She took up the axe which Roy had left behind him, and went into the forest behind the hut to cut firewood. She was very expert at this laborious work. Her blows were indeed light, for her little arms, although strong for their size, were not strong for such labour; but she knew exactly where to hit and how to hit. Every stroke fell on the right spot, with the axe at the right angle, so that a chip or two flew off every time. She panted a good deal, and grew uncommonly warm, but she liked the work; her face glowed and her eyes sparkled, and it was evident that she was not exhausted by it. In little more than an hour she had cut enough of dry wood to make a fire that would have roasted an entire sheep. Then she carried it to the hut, after which she sat down to rest a little.

While resting, she gathered carefully together all the scraps of food in the hut, and found that there was still enough for two good meals; so she ate a small piece of dried fish, and began to wish that Roy would return. Suddenly she was startled by a loud fluttering noise close to the hut, and went out to see what it could be.

It might be supposed that a little girl in such solitary and unprotected circumstances would have felt alarmed, and thought of wolves or bears; but Nelly was too well accustomed to the dangers and risks of the backwoods to be much troubled with mere fancies. She was well aware that wolves and bears, as a rule, shun the presence of human beings, and the noise which she had heard was not of a very alarming character.

The first sight that greeted her was a large bird of the grouse species, sitting on a tree not three yards from the hut. She almost felt that by springing forward she could seize it with her hands, and her first impulse was to throw the axe at it; but, checking herself, she went noiselessly back into the hut, and quickly reissued with the bow and a couple of arrows.

Fitting an arrow to the string, she whispered to herself, "Oh, how I *do* hope I won't miss it!" and took a careful aim. Anxiety, however, made her hand unsteady, for, the next moment, the arrow was quivering in the stem of the tree at least three inches below the bird.

A look of deep disappointment was mingled with an expression of determination as she pursed her little mouth and fitted the second arrow to the string. This time she did not take so careful an aim, but let fly at once, and her shaft entered the bird's throat and brought it to the ground. With a cry of delight she sprang upon her prize, and bore it in triumph into the hut, where she speedily plucked it. Then she split it open, and went down to the lake and washed it quite clean and spread it out flat. Her next proceeding was to cut a short stick, about two feet in length, which she pointed at both ends, making one point thinner than the other. This thin point she thrust through the bird, and stuck it up before the fire to roast, placing a small dish, made of birch bark, below it to catch the dripping.

"I hope he won't come back till it's ready," she muttered, as the skin of the bird began to brown and frizzle, while a delicious odour began to fill the hut.

Just as the thought was uttered, a footstep was heard outside, the covering of the doorway was raised, a tall figure stooped to enter, and the next instant a gaunt and half-naked savage stood before her.

Nelly uttered a faint cry of terror, but she was so paralysed that she could make no effort to escape, even had escape been possible.

The appearance of the Indian was indeed calculated to strike terror to a stouter heart than that of poor Nelly; for besides being partially clad in torn garments, his eyes were sunken and bloodshot, and his whole person was more or less smeared with blood.

As the poor child gazed at this apparition in horror, the Indian said, "Ho!" by way of salutation, and stepping forward, took her hand gently and shook it after the manner of the white man. A gleam of intelligence and surprise at once removed the look of fear from Nelly's face.

"Wapaw!" she exclaimed breathlessly.

"Ho!" replied the Indian, with a nod and a smile, as he laid aside his gun and snowshoes, and squatted himself down before the fire.

There was not much to be gathered from "ho!" but the nod and smile proved to Nelly that the intruder was indeed none other than her old friend Wapaw.

Her alarm being now removed, she perceived that the poor Indian was suffering both from fatigue and wounds — perhaps from hunger too; but this latter idea was discarded when she observed that several birds, similar to the one she had just killed, hung at the Indian's belt. She rose up quickly, therefore, and, running down to the lake, soon returned with a can of clear water, with which she purposed bathing Wapaw's wounds. Wapaw seized the can, however, and emptied the contents down his throat, so she was constrained to go for a second supply.

Having washed the wounds, which were chiefly on the head and appeared to her to be very severe, although, in reality, they were not so, she set the roasted bird before him and desired him to eat.

Of course she had put a great many questions to Wapaw while thus occupied. Her residence with the Indians had enabled her to speak and understand the Indian tongue a little, and, although she had some difficulty in understanding much of what Wapaw said in reply, she comprehended enough to let her know that a number of white men had been killed by the savages, and that Wapaw was fleeing for his life.

On first hearing this a deadly paleness overspread her face, for she imagined that the white people killed must be her own kindred; but Wapaw quickly relieved her mind on this point.

After this he devoted himself entirely to the roasted bird, and Nelly related to him, as well as she could, the particulars of her own and Roy's escape from the Indians.

CHAPTER XX.

More Surprising Discoveries.

While they were thus occupied, a cry was heard to ring through the forest. The Indian laid his hand on his gun, raised his head, which he turned to one side in a listening attitude, and sat as still as a dark statue. The only motion that could be detected in the man was a slight action in his distended nostrils as he breathed gently.

This attitude was but momentary, however, for the cry was repeated ("Hi! Nelly, hi!") in clear silvery tones, and Wapaw smiled as he recognised Roy's voice, and quietly resumed his former occupation.

Nelly bounded up at once, and ran out to receive her brother, and tell him of the arrival of their old friend.

She slipped on her snowshoes, and went off in the direction of the cry. On rounding the foot of a cliff she discovered Roy, standing as if he had been petrified, with his eyes glaring at the snow with a mingled look of surprise and alarm.

Nelly's step roused him.

"Ho! Nell," he cried, giving vent to a deep sigh of relief, "I'm thankful to see you — but look here. What snowshoe made *this* track? I came on it just this moment, and it pulled me up slick, I can tell ye."

Nelly at once removed Roy's alarm, and increased his surprise by telling him of the new arrival, who, she said, was friendly, but she did not tell him that he was an old friend.

"But come, now, what have you got for dinner, Roy?" said Nelly, with an arch smile, "for oh! I'm *so* hungry."

Roy's countenance fell, and he looked like a convicted culprit.

"Nell, I haven't got nothin' at all."

"*What* a pity! We must just go supperless to bed, I suppose."

"Come, lass, I see by the twinkle in your eye that you've got grub somehow or other. Has the redskin brought some 'at with him?"

"Yes, he has brought a little; but the best fun is that I shot a bird myself, and had it all ready beautifully cooked for your supper, when Wap —"

"Well, what d'ye mean by Wap?" inquired Roy, as Nelly stopped short.

"Nothing. I only meant to say that the Indian arrived suddenly, and ate it all up."

"The villain! Well, I'll pay him off by eatin' up some o' *his* grub. Did he say what his name was, or where he came from?" inquired Roy.

"Never mind, you can ask him yourself," said Nelly, as they drew near to the hut; "he seems to me to have been badly wounded by his enemies."

They stooped and entered the hut as Nelly spoke. The Indian looked up at her brother, and, uttering his wonted "Ho!" held out his hand.

"Good luck to ye!" cried Roy, grasping it and shaking it with a feeling of hearty hospitality. "It's good to see yer face, though it *is* a strange un; but – hallo! – I say – yer face ain't so strange, after all! – what! Why, you're not Wap – Wap – Wapaw!"

The Indian displayed all his teeth, which were very numerous and remarkably white, and nodded his head gently.

"Well now, that beats everything!" cried Roy, seizing the Indian's hand again and shaking it violently; then, turning to Nelly, he said, "Come, Nell, stir yer stumps and pluck two o' them birds. I'll split 'em, an' wash 'em, an' roast 'em, an' we'll all eat 'em – Wapaw'll be ready for more before it's ready for him. Jump, now, and see if we don't have a feast tonight, if we should starve tomorrow. But I say, Wapaw, don't ye think the redskins may be after you yet?"

The first part of this speech was uttered in wild glee, but the last sentence was spoken more earnestly, as the thought occurred to him that Wapaw might have been closely pursued, for Nelly had told him of the Indian having been wounded by enemies and obliged to fly.

Wapaw shook his head, and made his young friend understand as well as he could that there was little chance of that, as he had travelled with the utmost speed in order to distance his pursuers, and induce them to give up the chase.

"Well, it may be as you say, friend," observed Roy, as he sat down before the fire and pulled off his hunting mocassins and socks, which he replaced by lighter foot-gear more suited to the hut; "but I don't much like the notion o' givin' them a chance to come up and cut all our throats at once. It's not likely, however, that they'll be here tonight, considerin' the pace you say you came at, so we'll make our minds easy, but with your leave we'll cut our sticks tomorrow, an' make tracks for Fort Enterprise. We han't got much in the way o' grub to start wi', it is true, but we have enough at least for two days' eatin', and for the rest, we have our guns, and you to be our guide."

This plan was agreed to by Wapaw, who thereupon advised that they should all lie down to sleep without delay. Roy, who was fatigued with his day's exertions, agreed, and in less than half an hour the three were sound asleep.

Next morning they arose with the sun, much refreshed; and while Wapaw and Nelly collected together and packed on their new sledge the few things that they possessed, Roy went for the last time to cast his line in Silver Lake. He was more fortunate than usual, and returned in an hour with four fine fish of about six pounds' weight each.

With this acceptable, though small, addition to their slender stock of provisions, they left the hut about noon, and commenced their journey, making a considerable *détour* in order to avoid meeting with any of the Indians who might chance to have continued the pursuit of Wapaw.

That same evening, towards sunset, a party of hunters marched out of the woods, and stood upon the shores of Silver Lake, the tracks about which they began to examine with particular interest. There were six of the party, five of them being white hunters, and one an Indian. We need scarcely add that they were our friend Robin and his companions.

"I tell 'ee what it is," cried Robin, in an excited tone, "that's my Nelly's fut; I'd know the prints o't among a thousand, an' it's quite plain Roy is with her, an' that Wapaw has come on 'em, for their tracks are clear."

"Sure it looks like it," observed Larry O'Dowd, scratching his head as if in perplexity, "but the tracks is so mixed up, it ain't aisy to foller 'em."

"See, here's a well-beaten track goin' into the wood!" cried Walter, who had, like his companions, been searching among the bushes.

Every one followed Walter, who led the way towards the hut, which was finally discovered with a thin, scarcely perceptible line of smoke still issuing from the chimney. They all stopped at once, and held back to allow Robin to advance alone. The poor man went forward with a beating heart, and stopped abruptly at the entrance, where he stood for a few seconds as if he were unable to go in. At length he raised the curtain and looked in; then he entered quickly.

"Gone, Walter, they're gone!" he cried; "come in, lad, and see. Here's evidence o' my dear children everywhere. It's plain, too, that they have left only a few hours agone."

"True for ye, the fire's hot," said Larry, lighting his pipe from the embers in testimony of the truth of his assertion.

"They can't be far off," said Slugs, who was examining every relic of the absent ones with the most minute care. "The less time we lose in follerin' of 'em the better — what think ye, lad?" The Black Swan nodded his approval of the sentiment.

"What! without sleep or supper?" cried Stiff, whose enthusiasm in the chase had long ago evaporated.

"Ay," said Robin sternly, "*I* start *now*. Let those stop here who will."

To do Stiff justice, his objections were never pressed home, so he comforted himself with a quid of tobacco, and accompanied Robin and his men with dogged resolution when they left the but. Plunging once more into the forest, they followed up the track all night, as they had already followed it up all day.

CHAPTER XXI.

A Gladsome Meeting.

Some hours before dawn Robin Gore came to an abrupt pause, and looking over his shoulder, held up his hand to command silence. Then he pointed to a small mound, on the top of which a faint glow of light was seen falling on the boughs of the shrubs with which it was crowned.

The moon had just set, but there was sufficient light left to render surrounding objects pretty distinct.

"That's them," said Robin to Walter, in a low whisper, as the latter came close to his side; "no doubt they're sound asleep, an' I'm puzzled how to wake 'em up without givin' 'em a fright."

"Musha! it's a fright that Wapaw will give *us*, av we start him suddenly, for he's murtherin' quick wi' his rifle," whispered Larry.

"We'd better hide and then give a howl," suggested Stiff, "an', after they're sot up, bring 'em down with a familiar hail."

The deliberations of the party were out short and rendered unnecessary, however, by Wapaw himself. That sharp-eared red man had been startled by the breaking of a branch which Larry O'Dowd chanced to set his foot on, and, before Robin had observed their fire, he had roused Roy and Nelly and hurried with them to the summit of a rocky eminence, from which stronghold they now anxiously watched the proceedings of the hunters. The spot to which they had fled for refuge was almost impregnable, and might have been held for hours by a couple of resolute men against a host of savages.

Robin, after a little further consultation, resolved to send the Black Swan in advance to reconnoitre. This he did, contrary to his wonted custom of taking the lead in everything, because of an unaccountable feeling of dread lest he should not find his children there.

Black Swan at once stepped cautiously forward with his rifle, ready cocked, in the hollow of his left arm, and his finger on the trigger-guard. Step by step he moved towards the encampment without making the slightest noise, and with so little motion that he might easily have been mistaken for a dark shadow. Raising his head over the edge of the encampment he gazed earnestly into it, then he advanced another pace or two, finally he stepped into it, and, standing erect, looked around him. With a wave of his hand he summoned his comrades to advance. Robin Gore's heart beat hard as he approached, followed by the others.

Meanwhile they were closely watched by Roy and Wapaw. When the Black Swan's head appeared, Roy exclaimed in a whisper, "An Injun — d'ye know him, Wapaw?"

"He is one of our tribe, I think," replied the Indian, in the same low voice, "but I know him not; the light of the fire is not strong."

"If he's one o' your tribe," said Roy, "it's all up with us, for they won't be long o' findin' us here. Keep close to me, Nell. I'll stick by you, lass, don't fear."

Wapaw's brows lowered when he saw the Black Swan step into the encampment, and make the signal to his comrades to advance. He raised his rifle, and took deliberate aim at his heart.

"Roy," he whispered, "get an arrow ready, aim at the next man that steps into the light and let fly; I'll not fire till after you, for the smoke would blind you."

Roy obeyed with a trembling hand. Notwithstanding the rough life he had led in those wild woods of the West, he had never yet been called on to lift his hand against a human being, and the thought of taking life in this deliberate and almost murderous way caused him to shudder; still he felt that their case was desperate, and he nerved himself to the deed.

Another moment, and Robin stood beside the Black Swan. Roy tried to raise his bow, but his heart failed him. Wapaw glanced at him, and said sternly —

"Shoot first."

At that moment Obadiah Stiff stepped into the encampment, and, stirring the embers of the fire with a piece of stick, caused a bright flame and showers of sparks to shoot upwards. This revealed the fact that some of the party were white men, so Wapaw lowered his rifle. A single glance of his practised eye told him who they were. Laying his hand suddenly and heavily on Roy's shoulder he pressed him down.

"Come, let us go," he said quickly; "I must see these men alone, and you must keep close — you *must not look.*"

He said the latter words with emphasis; but in order to make sure that they should not have a chance of looking, he led his young companions to a point whence the encampment could not be seen, and left them there with strict injunctions not to quit the spot until he should return.

In a few seconds Wapaw stepped into the circle of light where Robin and his party were all assembled, and so rapid and noiseless had his movement been, that he was in the midst of them almost before they were aware of his approach.

"Wapaw!" exclaimed Walter in surprise, "why, you seem to have dropped from the clouds."

"Sure it's a ghost ye must be," cried Larry. The Indian took no notice of these remarks, but turned to Robin, who, with a look of deep anxiety, said —

"Have 'ee seed the childer, Wapaw?"

"They are safe," answered the Indian.

"Thank God for that!" cried Robin, while a sigh of relief burst from him: "I believe ye, Wapaw, yer a true man an' wouldn't tell me a lie, would ye?"

The tone in which the hunter said this implied that the statement was scarcely a true index to his feelings, and that he would be glad to hear Wapaw assure him that he was indeed telling the truth. But this Indian was a man of truthfulness, and did not deem it necessary to repeat his assertion. He said, however, that he would go and fetch the children, and immediately quitted the camp. Soon after he returned with Roy and Nelly; he had not told them, however, who the strangers were.

When Roy first caught sight of his father he gave a shout of surprise, and stood still as if he were bewildered. Nelly uttered a wild scream, and rushed forward with outstretched arms. Robin met her more than half way, and the next moment folded his long-lost little one to his bosom.

CHAPTER XXII.

At Silver Lake once more.

It were needless to detail all that was said and done during the remainder of that night, or, rather, morning, for day began to break soon after the happy meeting narrated in the last chapter. It would require more space than we can afford to tell of all that was said and done; how Robin embraced his children over and over again in the strength of his love, and thanked God in the fervour of his gratitude; how Roy and Nelly were eager to relate all that had befallen them since they were carried away into captivity, in a much shorter time than such a long story could by any possibility be told; how Walter rendered the telling of it much more difficult by frequent interruptions with eager questions, which induced divergencies from which the tale-tellers forgot to return to the points where the interruptions occurred; how Larry O'Dowd complicated matters by sometimes volunteering anecdotes of his own, illustrative of points similar to those which were being related; how Slugs always cut these anecdotes short with a facetious poke in the ribs, which caused Larry to howl; how Stiff rendered confusion worse confounded by trying to cook some breakfast, and by upsetting the whole affair into the fire; and how the children themselves broke in on their own discourse continually with sudden and enthusiastic questions as to the health of their mother and the welfare of the live stock at Fort Enterprise.

All this cannot be described, therefore we leave it to the vivid imagination of the reader.

"Now, comrades," said Robin, after the sun had risen, after breakfast had been and eaten, after every incident had been related at least twice over, and after every conceivable question had been asked four or five times — "now, comrades, it remains for us to fix what we'll do."

"To the Fort," said Larry O'Dowd abruptly.

"Ay — home!" cried Walter.

"Oh yes — home — home!" exclaimed Roy and Nelly in the same breath.

"Ditto," observed Obadiah Stiff.

Slugs and the Black Swan, being men of few words, said nothing, but nodded approval.

"Well, it's quite plain that we're all of one mind," resumed Robin; "nevertheless, there are one or two points to which I ax yer attention. In the first place, it's now near the end of November. Fort Enterprise, in a straight line, is more nor three weeks' march from hereaway. Our provisions is low. When I left the Fort provisions was low there too, an' if my brother Jeff ha'nt had more nor his usual luck in huntin' they'll be lower yet before long. Now, I think it would be better to go back to Silver Lake for a week or so, hunt an' fish there till we've got a good supply, make noo sleds, load 'em chock full, an' then — ho! for home. What say ye to that, comrades?"

As every one assented readily to this plan, they proceeded at once to carry it into execution. At first, indeed, Nelly looked a little disappointed, saying that she wanted to get to her darling mother without delay; but, on Walter pointing out to her that it would only delay matters a week or so, and that it would enable the whole party to rest and recruit, and give Wapaw time to recover thoroughly from his wounds, she became reconciled, and put on her snowshoes to return to Silver Lake with some degree of cheerfulness; and when, in the course of that day's walk, she began to tell her father of all the beauties and wonders of Silver Lake, she was not only reconciled but delighted to return.

"O father!" said she, as they walked briskly through the forest, "you've no notion what a beautiful place Silver Lake is. It's so clear, and so — so — oh! I don't know how to tell you; so like the fairy places Walter used to tell us of, with clear water and high cliffs, and the clouds shining up at the clouds shining down, and two suns — one below and another above. And then the hut! we made it all ourselves."

"What! made the trees and all?" said Robin, with a smile.

"No, of course not the trees; but we *cut* the trees and piled 'em up, and spread the brush-wood, and — and — then the fish! we caught *such* big ones."

"How big, Nelly?"

"Oh, ever so big!"

"How big may that be?"

"Well, some were so long," (measuring off the size on her arm,) "an' some near as long as my leg — an' they were good to eat too — no good! you've no notion; but you'll see and taste 'em too. Then there's the shooskin'! Did you ever shoosk, father?"

"No, lass — leastways I don't remember, if I did."

"But you know what it is?"

"To be sure, Nelly; ha'nt I seed ye do it often on the slopes at Fort Enterprise?"

"Well, the shooskin' here is far, *far* better. The first time Roy did it he said it nearly banged all his bones to pieces — yes, he said he felt as if his backbone was shoved up into his brain; and I sometimes thought it would squeeze all my ribs together. Oh, it is *so* nice! You shall try it, father."

Robin laughed heartily at this, and remarked that he would be very glad to try it, though he had no particular desire to have his ribs squeezed together, or his backbone shoved up into his brain!

Then Nelly went on with great animation and volubility to tell of the trapping of the bear, and the snaring of rabbits, and the catching of fish, and of Roy's peculiar method of wading into the lake for ducks, and many other things.

Roy, meanwhile, entertained Walter and Larry O'Dowd with a somewhat similar account of their doings during the months of their residence in that wild region; and thus the journey was beguiled, so that the time seemed to pass on swallows' wings.

Towards evening the party approached the spot where Silver Lake had first burst upon the enraptured gaze of the wandering pair. As they drew near, Roy and Nelly hurried on in advance, and, mounting the fallen tree on which they had formerly rested, waved to the others to come on, and shouted for glee. And well might they shout, for the evening happened to be brighter and calmer, if possible, than the one on which they first saw the lake. The rolling clouds were whiter, too, and the waters looked more silvery than ever.

The exclamations of delight, and the looks of admiration with which the glorious scene was greeted by the hunters when they came up, gratified the hearts of Roy and Nelly very much.

"Oh, *how* I wish mother was here to see it!" cried Nelly.

"Ain't *that* a place for a king to live in, daddy?" said Roy, enthusiastically.

"So 'tis, lad, so 'tis — leastwise it's a goodish spot for a hunter. How say you, Slugs?"

Slugs smiled grimly, and nodded his head.

"Would the red man like to pitch his wigwam there?" said Robin, addressing the Black Swan.

"He has pitched his wigwam here before," replied the Black Swan softly. "When he first took the White Swan home to be his mate, he came to hunt here."

"Och! is it the honeymoon ye spint here?" broke in Larry. "Faix, it's a purty spot for courtin', and no mistake. Is that a beehive over there?" he added, pointing across the lake.

"Why that's our hut — our *palace*," cried Nell, with gleeful look.

"Then the sooner we get down to it, and have supper, the better," observed Walter, "for we'll have to work hard tomorrow."

"Come along, then," cried Robin, "an' go you ahead, Roy; beat the track, and show us the way."

Roy accepted the position of honour. Nelly followed him, and the whole band marched off in single file along the shores of Silver Lake. They soon reached the hut, and here again Nelly found many interesting points to dilate upon. She poured her words into willing and sympathetic ears, so that she monopolised nearly all the talk during the time that Larry O'Dowd was preparing supper.

When that meal was being eaten the conversation became more general. Plans were discussed as to the intended procedure on the morrow, and various courses of action fixed. After that, as a matter of course, the pipes came out, and while these were being smoked, only the talkative members of the party kept up the conversation at intervals. Roy and Nelly having exhausted all they had to say, began to feel desperately sleepy, and the latter, having laid her head on her father's knee, fell sound asleep in that position. Soon the pipes were smoked out, the fire was replenished, the blankets unrolled; and in a very brief period of time the whole party was in a state of happy unconsciousness, with the exception of poor Wapaw, whose wounds made him rather restless, and the Black Swan, whose duty it was to take the first watch; for it was, deemed right to set a watch, lest by any chance the Indians should have followed the hunters' tracks, though this was not probable.

Next morning Robin aroused the sleepers somewhat abruptly by shooting a grey hen with his rifle from the tent door.

"There's breakfast for you and me, Nelly, at any rate," remarked the hunter, as he went down to the lake to secure his bird.

"An' won't there be the bones and feathers for the rest of us?" observed Larry, yawning, "so we won't starve this day, anyhow."

In a few minutes every man was actively engaged in work of some sort or other. Robin and Walter prepared fishing-lines from some pieces of buckskin parchment; Black Swan and Slugs went out to cut wood for making sledges; Stiff repaired the snowshoes of the party, or rather assisted Nelly in this operation; and Larry attended to the preparation of breakfast. Wapaw was the only one who lay still, it being thought better to make him rest, and get strong for the approaching journey.

During the course of the day the lines were tried, and a good number of fish caught. Slugs also went off in search of deer, and returned in the evening with a large stag on his broad shoulders. This raised the spirits of the party greatly, and they feasted that night, with much rejoicing, on venison, marrowbones, and broiled fish!

Thus they spent their time for several days. One party went regularly every morning to fish in the ice-holes; another party roamed the woods, and returned with grouse, or rabbits, and sometimes with deer; while some remained, part of the day at least, in the hut, mending snowshoes and moccasins, and making other preparations.

In the midst of all this busy labour, the shoosking was not forgotten. One day Robin said to his little daughter, at breakfast, that as they had got nearly enough of provisions for the journey they would take a holiday and go and have a shoosk. The proposal was hailed with delight, and the whole party went off with the new sledges, and spent the forenoon in sliding and tumbling down the hills like very children.

At last everything was ready for a start. The provisions were tightly fastened on the sledges, which were to be drawn by each of the men in turn. Snowshoes were put on, guns and bows looked to and shouldered, and on a bright, frosty December morning the hunters left the hut, struck into the woods, and set out for Fort Enterprise.

At the top of the slope, beside the fallen tree, they stopped with one consent and gazed back; and there Nelly took her last sad look at Silver Lake, and sorrowfully said her last farewell.

CHAPTER XXIII.

The Happiest Meeting of All.

The snow was driving through the forests and over the plains of the North American wilderness; the wind was shrieking among the tree-tops, and whirling the drift in great clouds high up into the frosty air; and the sun was setting in a glow of fiery red, when, on the last day of the year, Robin Gore and his followers came to an abrupt halt, and, with one consent, admitted that "the thing was impossible."

"We can't do it, boys," said Robin, resting his rifle against a tree; "so it's o' no use to try. The Fort is good ten miles off, an' the children are dead beat —"

"No they ain't," interrupted Roy, whose tone and aspect, however, proved that his father's statement was true; "at least *I'm* not beat yet — I'm game for two or three hours more."

"Well, lad, p'raps ye are, but Nelly ain't; so we'll camp here, an' take 'em by surprise in the morning early."

Nelly, who had been carried on the backs of those who had broadest shoulders during the last dozen miles, smiled faintly when spoken to, and said she was "ve-y s'eepy!"

So they set to work in the usual style, and were soon comfortably seated in their snowy encampment.

Next morning before dawn Robin awoke them.

"Ho!" he cried, "get up, lads, look alive! A happy New Year to 'ee all, young an' old, red an' white. Kiss me, Nell, dear — a shake o' yer paw, Roy. An' it's a good New Year's day, too, in more ways than one, praise the Almighty for that."

The whole party was astir immediately, and that feeling of kindly brotherhood which usually pervades the hearts of men on the first day of a new year, induced them to shake hands heartily all round.

"You'll eat your New Year's dinner at home, after all," said Walter to Nelly.

"Sure, an' it's a happy 'ooman yer mother'll be this good day," said Larry, as he stirred up the embers of the fire, and blew them into a flame.

The kettle was boiled, and a good breakfast eaten, because, although it is usually the custom for hunters to start on their day's journey, and accomplish a good many miles of it before breakfast, they had consideration for Roy and Nelly, both of whom were still suffering a little from the fatigue of the previous day. They hoped to be at Fort Enterprise in about four hours, and were anxious to arrive fresh.

The sun was rising when they reached the top of a ridge, whence they could obtain a distant view of the Fort.

"Here we are *at home*, Nelly," said Robin, stooping down to kiss his child on the forehead.

"Darling, *darling* mother!" was all that poor Nelly could say, as she tried in vain to see the Fort though the tears which sprang to her eyes.

"Don't you see it, Nell?" said Roy, passing his arm round his sister's waist.

"No, I don't," cried Nelly, brushing the tears away; "oh, *do* let us go on!"

Robin patted her on the had, and at once resumed the march.

*   *   *

That morning Mrs. Gore rose from her bed about the saddest woman in the land. Her mind flew back to the last New Year's day, when her children were lost to her, as she feared, for ever. The very fact that people are usually more jocose, and hearty, and happy, on the first day of the year, was sufficient to make her more sorrowful than usual; so she got up and sighed, and then, not being a woman of great self-restraint, she wept.

In a few minutes she dried her eyes, and took up her Bible, and, as she read its blessed pages, she felt comfort — such as the world can neither give nor take away — gradually stealing over her soul. When she met her kinsman and his friends at breakfast she was comparatively cheerful, and returned their hearty salutation with some show of a reciprocal spirit.

"Jeff," said Mrs. Gore, with a slight sigh, "it's a year, this day, since my two darlings were lost in the snow."

"D'ye say so?" observed Jeff, as he sat down to his morning meal, and commenced eating with much voracity.

Jeff was not an unkind man, but he was very stupid. He said nothing more for some time, but, after consuming nearly a pound of venison steak, he observed suddenly —

"Wall, I guess it wor a bad business that — worn't it, missus?"

"It was," responded Mrs. Gore; and, feeling that she had no hope of meeting with sympathy from Jeff, she relapsed into silence. After a time, she said —

"But we must get up a feast, Jeff. It won't do to let New Year's day pass without a good dinner."

"That's true as gosp'l," said Jeff. "Feed up is my motto, always. It don't much matter wot turns up, if ye don't feed up yer fit for nothin'; but, contrairy-wise, if ye do feed up, why yer ready for anythin' or nothin', as the case may be."

Having given vent to this sentiment, Jeff finished his meal with a prolonged draught of tea.

"Wall, now," said he, filling his pipe, "we've got enough o' deer's meat an' other things to make a pretty fair feast, missus, but my comrades and we will go an' try to git somethin' fresh for dinner. If we git nothin' else we'll git a appetite and that's worth a good long march any day; so, lads, if —"

Jeff's speech was interrupted here by a sudden and tremendous outburst of barking on the part of the dogs of the establishment. He sprang up and hastened to the door, followed by his companions and Mrs. Gore.

"Injuns, mayhap; see to your guns, boys, we can niver be sure o' the reptiles."

"They're friendly," observed one of Jeff's friends, as they stood at the Fort gate; "enemies never come on in that straightforward fashion."

"Not so sure o' that," said Jeff. "I've seen redskins do somethin' o' that kind when they meant mischief; but, if my eyes ain't telling lies, I'd say there were white men there."

"Ay, an' young folk, too," remarked one of the others.

"Young folk!" exclaimed Mrs. Gore, as she shaded her eyes from the sun with her hand, and gazed earnestly at the band which was approaching.

Suddenly one of them ran a little in advance of the rest, and waved a handkerchief. The figure was a small one. A faint cheer was heard in the distance. It was followed, or rather accompanied, by a loud, manly, and well-known shout.

Mrs. Gore grew pale, and would have fallen to the ground had not Jeff caught and supported her.

"Why, I *do* declare it's Robin — an' — eh! if there beant the children wi' 'im!"

The advancing party broke into a run as he spoke, another loud cheer burst forth, and in a few seconds Nelly was locked once more in her dear mother's arms.

CHAPTER XXIV.

Conclusion.

It is not necessary to say that there was joy — powerful, inexpressible — within the wooden walls of Fort Enterprise on that New Year's morning, and a New Year's hymn of praise welled up continually from the glad mother's heart, finding expression sometimes in her voice, but oftener in her eyes, as she gazed upon the faces of her dear ones, the lost and found.

The flag at Fort Enterprise, which had not flaunted its red field from the flagstaff since the sad day — that day twelve months exactly — when the children were lost, once more waved gaily in the frosty air, and glowed in the beams of the wintry sun. The sound of joyful revelry, which had not been heard within the walls of the Fort for a long, long year, once again burst forth with such energy that one might have been led to suppose its being pent up so long had intensified its power.

The huge fireplace roared, and blazed, and crackled, with a log so massive that no other Yule log in the known world could have held a candle to it; and in, on, and around that fire were pots, pans, and goblets innumerable, all of which hissed, and spluttered, and steamed at Larry O'Dowd, as if with glee at the sight of his honest face once again presiding over his own peculiar domain. And the parlour of Fort Enterprise — that parlour which we have mentioned as being Robin's dining-room and drawing-room, besides being his bedroom and his kitchen — was converted into a leafy bower by means of pine branches and festooned evergreens, and laid out for a feast the like of which had not been seen there for many a day, and which was transcendently more magnificent than that memorable New Year's day dinner which had been cooked, but not eaten, just three hundred and sixty-five days before.

In short, everything in and about Fort Enterprise bore evidence that its inmates meant to rejoice and make merry on that first day of a new year, as it was meet they should do under such favourable circumstances.

Jeff Gore had shot a deer not many days before, and one of its fat haunches was to be the great dish of the feast; but Robin said that it was not enough: so, after the first congratulations were over, he and Walter, and Slugs, and Black Swan, set off into the forest, and ere long returned with several brace of grouse, and a few rabbits. Roy, with a very sly look, had asked leave to go and have a walk on snowshoes in the woods with Nelly before dinner, but his father threatened to lock him up in the cellar, so he consented to remain at home for that day and assist his mother.

"Now, Nelly, you and Roy will come help me to prepare the feast," said Mrs. Gore, whose eyes were swollen with joyful weeping till they looked like a couple of inflamed oysters; "not that there's much to do, for, now that Larry is come back, we'll leave everything to him except the pl–plum — poo — poo — ding — oh! *my* darling!"

Here Mrs. Gore broke down for the fifteenth time, and, catching Nelly to her bosom, hugged her.

"Darling mother!" sighed Nelly.

"Och! but it's a sight good for sore eyes, anyhow," exclaimed Larry, looking up from his occupation among the steaming pots and pans.

Wapaw, who was the only other member of the party who chose to remain in the house during the forenoon of that day, sat smoking his pipe in the chimney corner, and regarded the whole scene with that look of stoical solemnity which is peculiar to North American Indians.

"Come, I say, this'll never do, mother," cried Roy, going to the flour-barrel which stood in a corner. "If we're to help you wi' that 'ere poodin', let's have at it at once."

Thus admonished, Mrs. Gore and her recovered progeny set to work and fabricated a plum-pudding, which was nearly as hard, almost as heavy as, and much larger than a sixty-four pound cannon ball. It would have killed with indigestion half a regiment of artillery, but it could not affect the hardened frames of these men of the backwoods!

In course of time the board was spread, the viands smoked upon it, and the united party set to work. Mrs. Gore sat at the head of the table, with Nelly on one side and Roy on the other. Robin sat at the foot, supported by the White Swan on his right, and Wapaw on his left. Ranged between these were Walter, Slugs, the Black Swan, Jeff Gore, Obadiah Stiff, the two other strangers who came with Jeff, and Larry O'Dowd — for Larry acted the part of cook only, and did not pretend to "wait." After he had placed the viands on the table, he sat down with the rest. These backwoodsmen ignored waiters. They passed their plates from hand to hand, and when anything was wanted by any one he rose to fetch it himself.

After the plates were cleared away, the tea-kettle was put on the table. In some parts of the backwoods spirits are (fortunately) so difficult to procure, that hunters and trappers live for many months without tasting a drop, and get into the habit of doing entirely without intoxicating drink of any kind. Robin had no spirits except animal spirits, but he had plenty of tea. When it was poured out into huge cups, which might have been styled small slop-basins, and sweetened and passed round, Robin applied his knuckles to the table to command silence.

"Friends," said he, "I niver wos much o' a speechifier, but I could always manage to blurt out my meanin' somehow. Wot I've got to say to you this day is, I'm thankful to the Almighty for givin' me back my childer, an' I'm right glad to see ye all under my roof this Noo Year's day, and so's the wife, *I* know — ain't ye, Molly, my dear?"

To this appeal Mrs. G. replied with a hysterical ye-es, and an application of her apron to the inflamed oysters. Robin continued —

"Well, I'm sorry there ain't nothin' stronger in the fort to give 'ee than tea, but for my part I find it strong enough to keep up my spirits, an' yer all heartily welcome to swig buckets-full o' that. There is an old fiddle in the store. If any o' ye can scrape a tune, we'll have a dance. If not, why we'll sing and be jolly."

This speech was followed up by another from Obadiah Stiff, who, with a countenance of the deepest solemnity, requested permission to make a few brief observations.

"Friends," said he, turning the quid of tobacco which usually graced his right cheek into his left, "it's not every day a man's got a chance o' — o' wot I was agoin' to observe is, that men who are so much indebted to their much-respected host as — as (Nelly happened to sneeze at this point, and distracted Stiff's attention) as — yes, I guess we ha'nt often got the chance to chase the redskins, and — and. In short, without makin' an onnecessairy phrase about it — I'm happy to say that *I* can play the fiddle, so here's luck."

Mr. Stiff sat down abruptly and drained his cup at a draught.

"Pr'aps," said Larry, with a twinkle in his eye, "Mister Stiff would favour the company wi' a song before we commence to cut capers."

"Hear, hear!" from Walter.

"Hurrah!" from Roy.

Mr. Stiff cleared his throat and began at once. The tune was so dolorous, and the voice so unmusical, that in any other circumstances it would have been intolerable, but there were lines in it touching upon "good fellowship," which partially redeemed it, and in the last verse there was reference made to "home," and "absent friends," which rendered it a complete success, insomuch that it was concluded amid rapturous cheering, so true is it, as Walter observed, that, "one touch of nature covers a multitude of sins!"

"Let's drink to absent friends an' owld Ireland," cried Larry, filling his cup and pushing the kettle round.

This was drunk with enthusiasm and was followed by a succession of toasts and songs, which were drunk and sung not at the table, but round the fire, to which the party withdrew in order to enjoy their pipes more thoroughly. Then followed a number of anecdotes of stories — some true, some doubtful, and some fabricated — which were listened to with deep interest, not only by Roy and Nelly, but by the whole party, including the Indians, who listened intently, with faces like owls, although they did not understand a word that was said.

Many of these stories were so touching that poor Mrs. Gore's eyes became more inflamed and more oysterlike than ever. Nelly, too, became sympathetic, and her eyes were similarly affected.

When the evening was pretty well advanced, the violin was sent for and tuned, and Stiff turned out to be a very fair player of Scotch reels; so the party laid aside their pipes, cleared the floor, and began to dance.

It was rough but hearty dancing. Each dancer composed his own steps on the spur of the moment, but executed them with a degree of precision and violence that would have caused civilised dancing masters to blush with shame and envy. Mrs. Gore and Nelly danced too, weeping the while with joy, and so did the White Swan, but her performances were peculiar. She danced with a slowness of manner and a rigidity of person that are utterly indescribable. She looked as if all her joints had become inflexible, except those of her knees, and her arms hung straight down at her sides, while she pendulated about the floor and gazed at the rafters in deep solemnity.

How they did keep it up, to be sure! Men of the backwoods find it no easy matter to fatigue their muscles or exhaust their spirits, so they danced all night, and a considerable portion of next morning too. Long before they gave in, however, the females were obliged to retire. They lay down on their rude couches without taking the trouble to undress, and in a few moments after were sound asleep — Nelly locked in her mother's arms, with their two cheeks touching, their dishevelled hair mingling, and a few tears welling from their inflamed eyes, and mixing as they flowed slowly down their united noses. Sleeping thus, the mother dreamed of home, and Nelly dreamed of Silver Lake.

*　　　*　　　*

Reader, our tale is told. We have not space to tell of what befell Robin Gore and his family in after life, but we may remark, in conclusion, that although Robin stoutly refused to go back to civilisation, in the course of a few years civilisation considerately advanced to him, and the wild region, which was once a dense forest around Fort Enterprise, finally became (to Mrs. Gore's inexpressible joy) a flourishing settlement, in which were heard the sounds of human industry, and the tinkle of the Sabbath bell.

www.ingramcontent.com/pod-product-compliance
Lightning Source LLC
Chambersburg PA
CBHW022038170626
46808CB00003B/1266